In Muffled Night

D. ERSKINE MUIR

With an introduction by Curtis Evans

Moonstone Press

This edition published in 2021 by Moonstone Press
www.moonstonepress.co.uk

Introduction © 2021 Curtis Evans

Originally published in 1933 by Methuen & CO. Ltd, London

ISBN 978-1-899000-40-1
eISBN 978-1-899000-41-8

A CIP catalogue record for this book is available from the British Library

Text designed and typeset by Tetragon, London
Cover illustration by Jason Anscomb
Printed and bound by CPI Group (UK) Ltd, Croydon, CR0 4YY

Contents

Introduction

"Has anyone ever heard of the Sandyford Place mystery?"

—Detective Sir Henry Merrivale in
John Dickson Carr's *Seeing Is Believing* (1941)

"Now we have no wish to impugn the justice of either the Scotch jury or Lord
Deas... It is impossible, however, for us to believe, on the evidence before us,
that the prisoner left her home with the deliberate intention of killing Jessie
M'Pherson, and almost as difficult to credit that the crime was committed by her,
alone and unassisted. An awful mystery still hangs over this strange tragedy..."

—editorial in the (Dublin) *Freeman's Journal*, 25 September 1862

"Every writer has a favorite child—Dickens has told us that his was David
Copperfield—and of all my naughty progeny there is none I prefer to the much
wronged heroine of the Sandyford Mystery. Old Fleming, too, is another of
my choicest characters... With his piety, his cunning and his cleaver, to say
nothing of his singular good luck, even the exclusive Lizzie Borden might have
been proud to have numbered him among her respected ancestors."

—Famed criminologist William Roughead in *Tales of the Criminous* (1956)

Nearly 160 years ago, on 7 July 1862, in the city of Glasgow, servant
Jessie McPherson was discovered dead at her master's home at 17
Sandyford Place in a ghastly welter of her own gore, the victim
of a deadly rain of forty vicious blows upon her head, face and
hands, which had been administered with an iron cleaver. Like
Abby Borden, the step-mother of notorious American accused
axe murderess Lizzie Borden, who was found brutally slain at her
home in the city of Fall River, Massachusetts, three decades later,
on 4 August 1892, Jessie McPherson had died from the proverbial
"forty whacks". (Lizzie Borden's slain father, so the famous morbid
children's jingle would have it, got one extra, making it "forty-one"

in his case.) In Glasgow the terrible crime at Sandyford Place quickly became the talk of the town, just as the dreadful double murder at Fall River soon set local tongues wagging. While in Fall River it was the respectable elder daughter of the house, Lizzie Borden, who was arrested and brought to trial, in Glasgow it was another servant upon whom the police alighted, a heretofore unoffending young married woman named Jessie McLachlan, the murder victim's closest friend. Both women were destined to become permanent denizens in the rogue's gallery of classic murder cases.

The chief witness against Jessie McLachlan at her murder trial in 1862 was James Fleming, the venerable patriarch of the Fleming household, where the late Jessie McPherson had been employed. Old Fleming, as he was dubbed to distinguish him from his son John, was, by his own account, eighty-seven years old—although others claimed he was merely seventy-eight. In either case, he was, judging by his familiar behaviour with his women servants, still a virile, if not a randy, old man. He had been alone in the house with the dead woman over that fatal weekend in July, but claimed he had not realized she was actually there, murdered. (The rest of the Flemings retired to the family's country house over the summer months, with John Fleming and his son, John, Jr., trekking to Glasgow to carry on business.) It proved that Jessie McLachlan had been present at the house too, although she lied about this at the trial, as well as about numerous other points, to her grave legal peril.

At the conclusion of the presentation of the cases of the prosecution and defence, the presiding judge, Lord Deas, inveighed against the defendant for no fewer than four hours. After the judge had concluded his damning summing-up, the jury retired for just fifteen minutes before delivering a verdict of guilty. But things were just getting started. At the pronouncement of the verdict, Jessie McLachlan had her counsel read a remarkable statement on her behalf, in which she implicated none other than Old Fleming as the murderer of Jessie McPherson. Evincing no hesitation in categorically dismissing the defendant's story as "wicked falsehoods", Lord Deas sentenced the unfortunate young woman to death by hanging. The resulting public outcry, however, led, seven weeks later, to the commutation of her sentence to a term of life imprisonment. As in the case of another notorious accused Victorian-era murderess, Florence Maybrick, a judicial system unable or unwilling to admit that a terrible mistake quite possibly had been made, settled upon ruining a woman's life rather than killing her outright as an acceptable expedient.

Jessie McLachlan was released from prison in 1877 and, like Florence Maybrick after her, left the United Kingdom for the United States, that haven of the tired, poor and arguably unjustly convicted, where she died in her sixties in 1899. Like Florence Maybrick and Lizzie Borden, Jessie's infamy lived after her, and for nearly 120 years after her death people have debated whether she really was guilty of murder, or whether the culprit might really have been that plausible old devil James Fleming. In 1911 forty-year-old Scottish lawyer William Roughead, who would become arguably the twentieth century's premier criminologist, edited *Trial of Mrs. M'Lachlan* for the Notable British Trials series. The case, which he dubbed "an ideal murder", obsessed him for the rest of his life, just as the Lizzie Borden mystery in Fall River bewitched his brilliant American counterpart, Edmund Lester Pearson. By the Golden Age of detective fiction the bloody killing at Sandyford Place had become one of the stars in the constellation of classic murders, with passing mentions of it being made in Dorothy L. Sayers' *Busman's Honeymoon* (1937), Gladys Mitchell's *When Last I Died* (1941) and John Dickson Carr's *Seeing Is Believing* (1941). Even more significantly it served as the basis for two thirties mystery novels, George Goodchild and Bechhofer Roberts' *The Dear Old Gentleman*, which appeared in 1935, and the novel that you have before you now, *In Muffled Night*, which was first published in 1933 by Dorothy Agnes Sheepshanks Muir (1889–1977), under her pseudonym D. Erskine Muir.

The author turned to writing professionally after the unexpected death in 1932 of her husband, Thomas Arthur Erskine Muir, leaving her with the onerous task of raising two young children alone in Depression-era England. Under her deliberately sexually ambig-uous pen name, the Oxford-educated writer (she graduated from Somerville College, like Dorothy L. Sayers, who was four years her junior) published both works of European history, like *Prussian Eagle* (1940) and *Machiavelli and His Times* (1936)—the latter of which, on its publication in the United States, was favourably critiqued on the full front page of the *New York Times Book Review*—and a trio of accomplished detective novels: *In Muffled Night* (1933), which was possibly inspired by her late husband's Scottish ancestry, *Five to Five* (1934) and *In Memory of Charles* (1941). In all three of these detective novels, Muir ingeniously employed true crimes as the basis for her plots, artfully spinning original solutions to some of the most baffling conundrums in the history of human slaugh-ter. Unfortunately, her creative essays in crime fiction were never published in the United States and memory of them soon faded in the United Kingdom, despite the critical praise which they had garnered from such authorities on the fine art of murder as Dorothy L. Sayers. We owe Moonstone Press a great debt of gratitude for wiping the obscuring dust from these finely wrought jewels of crime fiction.

When you read *In Muffled Night*, will you beat Detective-Inspector Woods—"a man of about 36, not at all resembling the stolid matter-of-fact man of routine", but rather "highly intelligent, and of the imaginative, introspective type"—to the solution of the brutal murder of Helen Bailey, housekeeper at "The Towers" to the well-off, highly respectable Murrays of London, headed by "old" James Murray, that imperious widower of sixty-eight? Who done it, you ask? I'll no' be tellin'! As the great mystery writer Christianna Brand put it in the title of her Edgar-nominated 1960 study of the bizarre McPherson murder, *Heaven Knows Who*.

CURTIS EVANS
Germantown, TN
26 May 2021

CHARACTERS

JAMES MURRAY. Aged 68. Born 1865. Married 1885.

JOHN MURRAY, his son. Aged 47. Born 1886. Married 1914.

ALAN MURRAY, son of John. Aged 18.

GLENDA MURRAY, daughter of John. Aged 17.

HELEN BAILEY, housekeeper to the Murrays.

MARY SPENS.

JACK SPENS, husband of Mary.

ELEANOR SPENS, sister to Jack.

SUPERINTENDENT GOWING, of Scotland Yard.

DETECTIVE-INSPECTOR WOODS.

MRS. HUGHES.

JOHN RAWLINGS.

NOTE

All the above characters are fictitious and have no
reference to any living person or persons.

PLAN OF FIRST FLOOR SUITE AT "THE TOWERS"

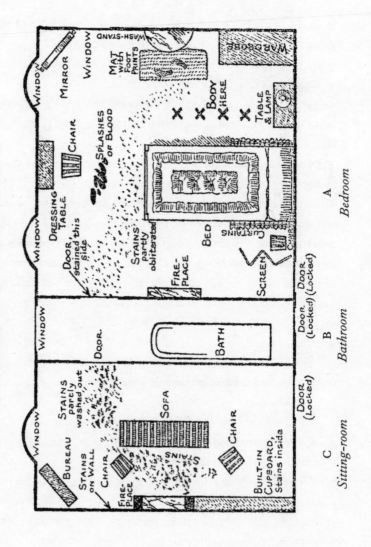

C
Sitting-room

B
Bathroom

A
Bedroom

Chapter I

THE PERSONS

"Mere mischance and plots and errors happen"

Hamlet.

I t was not at all a suitable house for a murder. Of course there have been murders in the houses of the good and great. But "The Towers" seemed the embodiment of everything peaceful, sober, and respectable. It was a large house, on the Highstead Heights, above London, surrounded with big gardens, with glass-houses, a carriage-drive, a shrubbery, a small wood, and every appurtenance of the rich, solid, middle-class. The mid-Victorians who built it, furnished it and lived in it, would always have felt that anything in the nature of a brutal bloodstained crime could not, in conformity with divine and natural law, be associated with such a house. Even in the present day it had, owing to a series of rather peculiar circumstances, retained the atmosphere with which it had been impregnated by its first owners.

Still furnished in the style of the eighteen-eighties, the scheme of decoration seemed almost incredible to the modern young. A specimen of the modern girl might, and in fact did, feel extremely out of her element on entering this house. Diana Ford was of this species, and staying in the house for the first time, as a totally unprepared visitor, she came down to breakfast and entered the dining-room feeling akin to 'stout Cortez when with eagle eyes he star'd', and had she but had a companion they would have emulated that famous band and 'looked at each other with a wild surmise'. As it was, she could only gaze round the room with a feeling of complete stupe-faction. Never had she seen such a room, or thought it possible that so complete a relic could remain unspoilt and untouched, and she stood looking about her and taking in its details with much amuse-ment. She had read, in common with everyone else, reconstructions of the mid-Victorian scene. She had even visited a model museum whose period-rooms included one with the setting of the eighteen-eighties. Nothing, however, had forewarned her that she could one day actually sit down in a room still used for ordinary daily life and yet in itself an exact survival of those past days.

It was rather a dark room. The heavy sash windows had their lower frames filled with squares of coloured glass. The buff blinds were neatly drawn down about a foot. Even such light as could enter through the restricted space thus left, had first to filter through deep cream lace curtains, hanging from the top of the high windows in billowing folds to the floor. Completing this stout resistance against the sunlight were long thick curtains in a sort of rep material and of a deep-red tone, with vast red ropes catching in their swelling waists.

The carpet, also red, was very thick and soft, and stretched across the floor right up to the wainscot of the walls. Those walls were papered in the same slightly ominous shade of crimson. 'Flock-paper' thought Diana, with vague ideas of her readings floating through her mind, "that, I think, must be flock".

Large oil paintings, mostly landscapes, but including also scenes with fishing-boats, ducks on a pond, a village street, all heav-ily framed in gold, loomed from the walls. In one corner a full-sized statue of a woman in white marble leaned out into the room. In another a marble child lay asleep on a frilled marble cushion, 'brought from Rome on a wedding trip'.

A sofa and two large arm-chairs and the heavy mahogany set of dining-room chairs were covered with what Diana mentally described as 'carpet material', by which term she meant a kind of velvet plush with a geometrical pattern in shades of drab, dark blue, and maroon.

The mantelpiece was of heavy black marble, grained with white. At either end of it stood a tall Doric column in buff marble, copies of some pillars in a famous Grecian temple. In the middle stood a large black marble clock, inlaid with malachite, and with the bronze figure of a draped woman sprawling across the top. Two Satsuma vases, one on either side of the clock, completed the array.

From the old-fashioned china bell-knob at the side dangled a placard, illuminated in heavy silver lettering, "Christ is the Head of this house, the Unseen Guest at every meal, the silent Listener to every conversation."

"Well," thought Diana, "I hope we all live up to that—though, after all," she reflected, "I expect psycho-analysts think of our subconscious as a sort of listener to everything we say too."

As far as she had seen, the whole house was the same. The staircase, which she had descended, was painted a deep brown, both walls and woodwork, and carpeted in brown of a lighter shade. The fat pillars which supported the roof of the hall were also painted dark brown. Brown velvet curtains hung from the great staircase window. More statues stood at the turn of the stairs, and one window was extended into a fernery.

Her bedroom had been chiefly filled with an immense bedroom suite, in walnut, every leg and possible support being a twirling spiral. The bed was a half-tester bed, with a canopy overshadowing the pillows, and both bed and window had dark-green damask curtains. The carpet was dark green, with bunches of pink and red roses. The dressing-table had white muslin petticoats over green, and the walls were hung with steel engravings after Poussin. The house seemed to be absolutely complete in the mid-Victorian style.

Hunger made Diana's thoughts turn towards the breakfast-table, which nobly maintained the Victorian tradition of comfort without stint. The white damask cloth came down almost to the floor. A large fat silver tea-pot, coffee-pot, and two or three jugs for milk and cream shone and glittered at one end. Vast cups and saucers were ranged before them. Two plates showed by the napkins emerging from their covers that hot scones lay within. On the sideboard four massive silver entrée dishes, ranged on a gigantic chafing dish, were flanked by a vast ham, while the back of the sideboard showed an immense array of silver trays, and salvers, cruets, and other objects.

A coal fire sparkled and glowed in the fireplace, for, in spite of being early July, a very wet, cold spell had overtaken London, and the reeking damp without made the warmth within very acceptable.

Diana, in whose own modern home greater ease compensated for less comfort and dignity, wondered how long she would have to wait before her hostess and friend appeared. She had come down on hearing the gong, and wondered why none of the household were on the scene. At this moment the door opened, and two men came in together. Diana had arrived so late the previous night that she had scarcely seen any of the family. She had been taken up to her room by her friend, and had hardly grasped who were the other inmates of the house. The two men who now came in were clearly father and son—and the elder she knew must be old Mr. James Murray, her friend Glenda's grandfather.

"Good morning, Miss Ford," said the younger of the two. "I don't think you saw my father last night? Father, this is Miss Ford, Glenda's friend." The older man came forward and shook Diana's hand, and she was aware of a tall, thin, keen-faced old man, who scrutinized her swiftly out of an extraordinarily piercing pair of blue eyes. But, before she had much time in which to contemplate her host, the door opened again and her own friend and contemporary, Glenda Murray, came hurrying in, followed by her brother Alan.

Glenda Murray was an extremely charming girl. She had inherited her grandfather's peculiar shade of blue eyes, but with her they were not piercing, but bright and sparkling. She was tall and fair, with rather an appealing face. Perhaps the restraint which old James Murray clearly imposed upon his family had checked her natural gaiety. Certainly she produced an effect of fragility and timidity, which is not very common nowadays. She was a girl who won the affections of others very easily, a characteristic which had some influence on forthcoming events. Her brother, Alan, resembled her, though he looked less delicate. His face showed intelligence, and the promise of character, but, at the moment, was spoilt by the sullen, downcast look with which he came up to the table. It was perfectly clear that he was not on good terms with his grandfather, and equally so that he was obliged to bear with the old man's imperious ways. James favoured Alan with a hostile glare, but otherwise vouchsafed him no greeting in reply to the mumbled "'Morning, Grandfather" forced from reluctant lips. The whole group were aware of impending unpleasantness, and the girl tried hastily to avert it.

"Oh," said Glenda, "Good morning, Diana, so you're down already. I am so sorry I wasn't up earlier. Good morning, Daddy, good morning, Grandfather. We're not really late, are we? Oh no, Helen's not here yet," in a tone of relief, glancing at the head of the table.

"I am rather late, I am afraid," said a voice behind her, and a woman came in, also rather hastily. "I am sorry, Mr. Murray,"—addressing the elder man—"but we have had a domestic upheaval. Mrs. Randall has had an accident, and I have had to send for the doctor, and we are all upside down and behindhand."

"Well, we won't wait further," came very testily from Mr. Murray. "I suppose this upheaval accounts for my having been called later than I should have been, about which I meant to complain. We will have no further delay, if you please." Then very imperiously, "Alan, kindly ring the bell for prayers." Alan did so, with a gloomy air, and then handed his grandfather a large Bible with long, dark-blue silk markers inserted at various places, which had been reposing on a side table.

James Murray sat down at the end of the table and opened the Bible. The family and their guests sat scattered near the fireplace, the maids filed in at the other end. Daily prayers were still the rule in that household. Diana, during the reading, surreptitiously took stock of her hosts. The three generations of Murrays showed very little signs of any close relationship, and in themselves represented rather aptly the changing world. When later events had made the members of this family, now quietly seated round their lavish breakfast-table, notorious throughout the length and breadth of the land, Diana often tried to recall the first impression they had made upon her that morning at "The Towers".

James Murray was clearly the dominating person in the household. His ways were obviously those to which everyone else had to conform. His strong personality made itself felt at once, and it was clear that to him was due the retention of the old-fashioned scheme of decoration and the old-fashioned way of life. He looked what indeed he was—a fierce old survivor of the late-Victorian age. To him was clearly to be attributed the religious strain which manifested itself in the continuance of daily prayers, and in the text hanging on the wall. He looked a hard man to cross, one who would make a bad enemy, and probably an exacting friend. He wore the old-fashioned dress of a well-to-do business man—black coat and waistcoat, dark trousers, and a black-and-white tie.

His son, John Murray, looked far more of the ordinary man of business. The most noteworthy thing about him was his very neat and natty appearance. He was extremely well dressed, in a dark suit, with a blue-striped shirt, blue tie, and smart socks and shoes. He seemed the only person indifferent to the undercurrent of uneasiness which made itself felt in the family circle. There was a certain air of steadiness and quiet self-confidence about him which gave the impression that here was a man who could be relied upon, and who was certainly not lacking in willpower, though compared with the old man he might superficially be adjudged to have less force. James impressed by something unusual and fierce in his appearance; John did not in the same way alarm, but a closer scrutiny would show an equal firmness of chin and jaw, though on the surface perhaps he had not his father's rugged characteristics. His face was intelligent, but of a more ordinary type. He looked efficient and placid. Young Alan, John's son, was slimmer, taller, and more delicately built altogether. He was slightly untidy in appearance, and his Fair Isle jumper and flannel trousers made him look as if he were meant for quite other activities compared with the stiff trimness of the other two. All three were alike in that they clearly came from a family which was accustomed to spend money freely, and to keep up a high standard of appearances.

Prayers over, James, unfolding his copy of *The Times*, glanced with considerable irritation at Alan, who was muttering something to Glenda in the window, but before the old man could say anything the dark-haired woman began to speak. James cut her short at once.

"We'll wait till breakfast is over, please, Miss Bailey, before we go into domestic difficulties. Now, children, stop that unnecessary chattering and we'll begin." His bad temper was obvious, and, with an accentuated feeling of constraint, all drew in their chairs and the meal began.

Diana, in the intervals of eating an extraordinarily large break-fast—for she found herself unequal to demanding an 'orange juice only' meal—pondered over her unusual surroundings. For that they were unusual was betokened by something besides the out-of-date decorations and furniture. Glenda Murray she had known at the school they had both but recently left. Alan, Glenda's eighteen-year-old brother, she had also met once or twice before. She was now on her way to stay with them at their country house near Lewes, but in order to break the journey from her Scottish home it had been arranged that she should spend the night at the Murrays' Highstead house. "It's our home in one sense," Glenda had explained on her arrival the night before, "though it's not our house. Grandfather lives here, with our old governess as housekeeper, and Daddy lives here too during the week and goes down to Red Barns at week-ends. Red Barns is Daddy's own house and we love it, but we have to be here a good deal with Grandfather. He won't let us go off altogether. Poor old Alan will have to be here practically all the time now he's pushed into the business instead of going up to Oxford." "And why 'poor'?" inquired Diana, who saw no hardship in stepping into a good business even if it entailed living in this house. "Oh, well"—and Glenda paused uncomfortably. "Well, to tell you the truth, Grandfather's a relic, and rather an unpleasant one, and not sufficiently a relic to be harmless. But you'll see for yourself," with an air of closing the subject, and she had said no more but left Diana to sleep. "Yes," reflected Diana, "Grandfather *is* rather unpleasant, I think," and her eyes sought out the face of the man seated at the end of the table. James Murray was about sixty-eight years old, but he looked less. Very tall, strongly built, with very thick, crisp grey hair, a long lean brown face, an eagle nose, and those still brilliant and very piercing blue eyes, suddenly flashing out from under drooping lids, he had that vague suggestion of a bird of prey which is always slightly unsettling to those who feel themselves to belong to the preyed-upon type. He had married young, having been left in command of a large fortune at the age of twenty, when both his parents were drowned in a famous wreck in the year 1885. He had stepped into his father's business, inherited the large house newly built by that father and furnished for the bride on her return from an Italian honeymoon, which accounted for the profusion of statues, actually brought from Rome as was fashionable in the 'eighties. James himself had married young, finding life lonely. He had refused to allow his very young bride to introduce any modern innovations into the rooms and decorations with which he was pleasingly familiar, and which in consequence remained as his mother had arranged them. Nor, after the death of his wife, had his only child, John, now a man of forty-seven, had any influence either in the house or in the business. So "The Towers" remained even in 1933 pretty much what it had been in 1885. Glenda told her friend afterwards that the whole house was furnished in the style of the rooms she had seen—every bedroom had a tester-bed, a fact with which every home in England was soon to be familiar. Indeed some of the points which were later to be argued and discussed in the columns of every daily paper turned on the entire lack of modernity about this household.

Yet, in the woman who had by now silently and swiftly poured out tea and coffee for the rather quiet subdued party, there seemed enough personality and strength to have changed even James Murray's household. Glenda's 'old governess' was old in the sense only of being her former governess. She was a woman of about forty, tall, slender and finely made. She was very dark, with almost black lustrous hair and a dark clear complexion. Her eyes were large, brilliant and of a very dark brown. Some kind of latent passion and power glowed behind the mask she had made of her face. "Ambition?" queried Diana to herself, and was not wholly satisfied, though sure that something unfulfilled, something strong and deep, lay there. So deeply interested was she in the personality of this woman she scarcely noticed the calm mild politeness of John Murray, next to whom she sat, and almost forgot the now negligible charms of the lighter-metalled Glenda and Alan. She was almost subconsciously aware of the flick of James Murray's blue glance passing over her to reach the still cold face of Helen Bailey, though quite aware of Helen's restrained impatience and wish for the meal to end. No one got up, however, until James himself rose and walked towards the fireplace, as a signal he had finished his meal and all might now relax.

"Well, Helen," and his sharp hard tones struck unpleasantly through the room. "What's wrong?"

"It's annoying," replied Helen, "and I don't quite know what we're to do. Mrs. Randall has fallen and broken her arm rather badly. Dr. Graham has been in to set it, and as she'll be useless for work for at least six weeks she must go home at once. We don't want to have to look after her here. I don't see any alternative."

"Well," again sharply, "I suppose you can get a temporary cook to take her place?"

"That is the difficulty. I can't get any one in time, I'm afraid. It's Friday, and the household were to go down to Red Barns this afternoon, if you remember. I was going down myself with them to set them to work and meant to leave you with Mrs. Randall for the week-end. I should have come back on Monday to close up the house here before you joined us all in the country. Now I really don't quite know what is best to be done."

James Murray had listened in growing displeasure to this domestic history, while Glenda and Alan both looked horrified. They knew well enough that their grandfather was in one of his autocratic moods, and they at once perceived their own plans for a pleasant week-end in the country were threatened. It was possible that either James would come with them or he would insist on their staying behind in Highstead. Glenda glanced across entreatingly at her father, who understood her appeal, and himself wishful to get away from the tyrannical old master of the house, and enjoy the peaceful atmosphere of his own country home, endeavoured to ease the situation.

"But you can manage without Mrs. Randall, I suppose, after all. The kitchen maid can carry on surely," he put in, fully aware of something beneath this domestic misfortune and anxious to ease the situation unobtrusively.

"No," said Helen, "that's the point. Kate was to go down with you to-day to Red Barns for this week-end to look after all of you, while Mrs. Randall was to cook for Mr. Murray with just a daily help to do the rooms he would be using. The others were all to come down to open up the whole of Red Barns for the big party next week. It really is very awkward."

"Come now," broke almost angrily from the older man. "Helen, you're here to prevent me being bothered in just this way. Send the maids to the country as you'd planned, and let the woman do the rough work. You can stay on instead of Mrs. Randall yourself for the week-end. You know you can cook better than any one I've ever known!" A certain inflexion, meant to be flattering or meant to be sarcastic, Diana could not satisfy herself which, was unmistakable. Unmistakable too the colour it brought to Helen's clear, dark cheek. She paused, seemed as if she would retort sharply, then turned abruptly, and as she went out spoke coldly but with decision,

"Very well. I will arrange that."

She had scarcely been gone a moment before there came a ring at the front door and an extremely lovely young woman came quickly into the dining-room. Greeted by the whole family with an outburst of surprise and pleasure, she smiled round at them all before advancing to say good morning to the severe master of the house. Ever afterwards Diana looked with a thrill on the picture which always sprang up before her mental vision when she thought of that meeting. For within a few weeks those two, the old man and the beautiful girl, were to be known through the length and breadth of the country, and indeed for years to come a sinister and dreadful interest would cling about their names.

This unexpected and quite charming visitor was Mary Spens, of whom Diana had often heard Glenda speak. She, and her parents before her, had been friends of the Murray family for many years. Mary herself had been left an orphan at a very early age, and she had in the old days shared Glenda's lessons and been almost like a sister. She had very little money of her own, and being of an independent nature had determined to earn her own living as soon as she could. Too badly off to afford the fees at Glenda's expensive boarding school, she had first gone to a day school, then trained to be a secretary. Before she had done much more than settle into her first post, she had become engaged to one of Glenda's distant cousins, Jack Spens. It had seemed an ideal marriage, for Jack was young, attractive, and quite well off. The young Murrays had perhaps given Diana the impression that Mary, whom they thought perfection, might have done better, but to the outward eye Mary seemed the very picture of a smart gay young married woman.

"Well, Mary, what brings you here at this early hour?" questioned James, looking with an almost benevolent smile at the girl standing beside him.

"I've come to see Helen about something very important, and I knew she'd be off to the country early to-day. You're all going down to Red Barns she told me yesterday."

"Well, she's busy at the moment, so sit down and tell me all your news. Helen'll be free directly to attend to you."

Diana inwardly marvelled at the friendliness of the tone, for Mary Spens was just the type of girl she would have expected James Murray, with his strict ideas, to denounce. She was young, looking not more than twenty-one or twenty-two, was dark, slim and very elegant. She was beautifully but unmistakably made up, even at that early hour, and had in every detail of her appearance an air of sophistication. Yet she and James were clearly on the best of terms. His attitude towards her was not exactly that of the elderly male flirt, he was too austere and dignified for that, but there was an unmistakable tinge of admiration in the glances he threw at her sparkling lovely face. Mary was clearly aware of this, and her whole manner showed that, secure in his liking, she felt none of the nervousness and deference his family displayed. Indeed, had Diana been more of a psychologist, she would have perceived that in this—to her—unexpected behaviour of James lay a hint that like so many stern, austere men his very harshness and severity were curbs imposed on a nature which needed them more than most.

Mary, sitting down on the sofa, to wait for Helen to be disengaged, rattled on, talking and laughing to everyone, and showing that she was indeed the friend of all the family—until, glancing at the clock, John Murray declared that he and Alan must be off to the office. James was to follow later, as he did not usually arrive at work so early as they did.

"I hope you and Helen will be comfortable enough, Father," he said, and added rather doubtfully, "don't you think perhaps after all we'd better all stay in town and not go down to the country until Helen's found a cook? I don't quite like the idea of you and she being left with no maids in the house to look after you."

Instantly James' face darkened. "Certainly not," he said sharply. "You know I can't stand all this ridiculous fuss and commotion over maids. We'll do perfectly well without for a day or two, and I'll have no change of plans."

John Murray still hesitated, but apparently saw that further efforts would only lead to more unpleasantness, for James had made up his mind. He turned away with a distinct shadow on his usually calm features, and, as Diana went upstairs to get ready for her own departure, she saw Mary knocking at Helen's bedroom door, while she turned to call gaily over her shoulder down to old James standing in the hall. "Don't you go out yet, Mr. Murray. I'll not be long, and I want to come and have a special talk with you." Diana felt a pang of envy at the sight of any one so beautiful, so gay, and so obviously able to please and attract everyone with whom she came in contact.

Yet, while before the family party at "The Towers", Mary Spens had seemed full of life and good spirits, she was really burning with angry unhappiness, and at another breakfast-table, not very far away, her behaviour had been the cause of some very scathing comments. In her own home she had entirely failed to please. Mary had, in reality, rushed straight to "The Towers" from a violent scene with her husband, and that same husband was now pouring out the story of his woes into the ears of his unmarried sister, to whom he had telephoned as soon as the door banged behind his wife.

"I tell you, Eleanor. Mary says she's sick of life with me, but I've had enough of it too—it's absolutely intolerable the way she goes on."

The woman who stood listening intently to him said nothing, and he continued:

"Debts and more debts, and no end to them. I've told her I can't and won't pay again. I've already stopped her using my name for credit, and yet she pays no attention. A fresh batch of bills in this morning. I just won't stand it a day longer!"

"That means disagreeable publicity, Jack."

"Not any more disagreeable than these infernal rows—and I thought a girl who'd never had much money would know how to be careful of what she was given."

"You wouldn't like people to know about these 'rows' as you call them, though; you don't want malicious gossip added to your other troubles, and people always are spiteful."

"It seems to me we've malicious gossip enough as it is with Mary always repeating everything to the Murrays. I tell you, Eleanor, she's perpetually there, passing on everything that goes on here, and they all back her up—Glenda and Helen Bailey, and even old Murray himself. She's gone round there now, and a fine tale she'll be telling, I'll be bound, to the old man."

"Yes, I've noticed Mary is always in high favour with him," was the reply, in a tone of rather bitter significance.

Apparently angered beyond self-control at some sting in this, Jack Spens burst out, "I'll tell you, Eleanor—though I didn't mean to let you know just yet—if the Murrays take her part now, Mary and I will separate. She's gone over there to get them to back her up and help her out of the hole she's got into, and I've told her if she chooses to go to them she can stay there. I've had too much—and she can see if they're as ready to support her altogether as they are to back her up against me."

As soon as the words were past his lips, he seemed to regret them, and he added quickly:

"But I don't want to talk about it any more. We've got to wait and see what Mary says when she comes back, if she condescends to come back! Anyway, I'm off to the Coulson's now, and must catch my train. See you when I get home Sunday night."

He rang off, and his sister, after putting down the receiver, turned away with a very troubled expression.

Chapter II

THE NIGHT

"When I know, but I protest, as yet I do not"

Richard III.

R ed Barns proved a delightful house, to Diana's relief. She had found herself thoroughly disliking "The Towers," and, as she stood at her bedroom window before dressing for dinner, with the clear cool air of the Downs blowing in upon her, she lazily tried to analyse her feelings. She was conscious of two things, or rather, as her mind dwelt on the various people with whom she had been brought in contact during the past twenty-four hours, she gradually became aware of an uneasiness touching her consciousness when she thought of James Murray himself and of his relations with his family. Coming as a complete stranger to him, he had struck very forcibly upon her imagination, and she was haunted by the feeling that there was something ominous in the intensity of his determination. It struck her, with a queer sense of the disagreeable, that this ageing man should have been able to check all advance and all change in his household; that he should have forced upon two succeeding generations the ways and the surroundings of an earlier day. It gave the sense of being imprisoned in the past, of a barrier raised to prevent the younger generation advancing into the new age.

It seemed clear enough, at the beginning of the evening, that Glenda and Alan, and even their father, rejoiced in having escaped from the old man's influence. Everyone was more cheerful, less constrained, and the general feeling was more peaceful. Yet the minds of both John and his children did turn back towards "The Towers" and the pair left there in solitude, and presently discord crept in upon them.

"I don't feel quite happy about Helen and your grandfather," said John Murray, in a pause towards the end of dinner. "I rather wish I'd insisted on your staying up there, Alan."

"I'm glad you didn't," replied Alan shortly. "Grandfather wasn't in a mood to want me there, and, when he's like that, nothing I do is right."

"Still," pursued John pensively, "I don't feel we ought to have left Helen there to manage everything single-handed. She's not been quite up to the mark lately, and she'll find it a bother having to run the house and try to find a cook quite single-handed, and make your grandfather comfortable."

"Well," said Glenda pacifically. "She gets on better with Grandfather than Alan and I do. They'll probably be quite amicable there by themselves, whereas, if Alan had stayed, Grandfather would have been on to him the whole time."

A shadow crossed John's face, and he glanced across at his son. "Yes, you've not got on well with your grandfather of late, Alan, and it is a pity, just when you're coming into the office with us."

The sullen, gloomy look returned to Alan's face. He was silent for a moment and then replied:

"That's why we don't get on. I don't see why Grandfather should force me to come into the office now. You'd always promised me I should go up to Oxford, and I do resent having to give it up. It's not as if it were necessary either—I'm not wanted in the business so urgently as all that."

"It's no good raising the matter again now, Alan," returned his father rather sternly. "We settled all this in the spring. Your grandfather insisted you should give up any idea of Oxford, and I didn't wish to oppose him further."

Alan shot a very angry glance across the table, and Diana realized the antagonism which the matter clearly raised between father and son.

"Yes, I know," he said, restraining himself with an effort. "I'd relied on you, of course, to back me up with Grandfather. I thought you'd have wanted me to get a bit of outside life before I shut myself up in the business, and I know you can't feel I'll be much use to you there yet."

"That'll do, Alan," returned his father firmly. "We've been into this before, and it's no use bringing it up again now. I've told you I don't intend to vex your grandfather over it, as he's so determined in the matter, and you must make the best of it. Don't let's talk of it any more, please." To show his wish to close the discussion, he got up from the table and fetched the cigarette box, which he handed to Diana.

"But I think," he added, "that we'd better just ring up Helen after dinner, Glenda, and have a word with her. I'd like to be sure they're comfortable and all that."

Glenda glanced out of the window, the curtains having been left undrawn till the light should fade. The rain had stopped, but low, ragged clouds were sweeping across the sky, and the tops of the Downs were shrouded in driving mist.

"Shall we have the drawing-room fire, Daddy?" she inquired. "It's so very dismal with this damp.'"

"Yes," answered John, abstractedly, "it would be more cheerful, I think."

The evening passed rather slowly. After dinner, John Murray went off to his study, and the three young people were left to themselves. It was too cold and damp to go out, as they had intended to do, Glenda having a special fondness for climbing the shoulder of the Downs in the evening. Without John, they had no four for bridge, and Alan, still slightly ruffled by his passage of arms with his father, buried himself in a book and left the two girls to talk. They sat peacefully over the fire and time slipped on unobserved. Some time after eleven o'clock, when they were beginning to think about bed, the telephone rang, and Glenda went into the hall to answer it. She came back to inquire of Alan where their father was, for it was he who was wanted.

"In his study, I imagine," replied Alan, without looking up.

"No, he's not, stupid," said Glenda. "Of course, I looked in there, but he's not there. Just go and see if he's gone upstairs."

Alan threw down his book and bounced out of the room. After a moment, he came running down the stairs. "No, he's not there, and the maids say he went across to the garage after dinner. He's probably tinkering with the car. I'll go and fetch him. Who is it wants him?"

"Oh, old Penrose wants to see him early to-morrow about those fields he's buying, and say he must know what time Daddy'll be in."

"All right, I'll ask him to hold on a minute," and he dashed out at the side-door with much energy. He was back again almost at once. "No good, he's taken the car and gone out. Tell old Penrose we'll give the message and Daddy'll ring up when he comes in."

Glenda returned to the telephone and dealt with Mr. Penrose and came back into the drawing-room, relieved that the little incident had seemed to break in upon Alan's gloom. "What on earth has Daddy gone out for?" she said. "He never said he was going, and it's an awful evening. He can't just have gone for a spin for pleasure."

"Oh! I don't know," replied Alan, quite cheerfully. "I think he was a bit bored with me and probably felt he didn't want our company. He's rather a passion for motoring by himself you know; he says it distracts his mind."

"What does he want to distract it from?" queried Glenda.

"Oh! I don't know. He fusses a good bit about the business nowadays, you know, though Lord knows he's no need to. I think when Grandfather gets into a bad mood he makes Dad's life rather a burden, and I daresay he felt I was going to be another source of aggravation, and he's gone to work off his feelings."

"Well," said Glenda, resolving inwardly that her father might as well have any small help she could give him, "I wonder if he rang up Helen before he went out, or if he'd like me to do it?"

"Look on the telephone pad; he'll have entered up a trunk call if he had one; he always does, you know."

Back went Glenda to the telephone-table in the hall, but she found no entry on the pad kept for the purpose.

"Alan," she called through the open door. "He didn't get on to Helen. Shall I have a shot, or will she have gone to bed, do you think? Shall I leave it till the morning?"

"Oh no," answered Alan, who was secretly sorry he had vexed his easy-going father. "I'd get on if I were you; Helen will hear the telephone from her bedroom; it's over the study. She won't be in bed yet, and I expect Daddy will be rather glad to know they're all right."

Accordingly, Glenda sat down and embarked on the task of getting through a trunk call. The others in the drawing-room sat listening to her efforts with the agreeable sense of comfort given by resting while others toil. After a longish interval, punctuated by 'Oh! thank you, try them again. Oh! can't you? Well, I'd rather you gave them another ring, please. Oh! is it? What can it be? You don't know? Oh well, thank you, I'll have to leave it,' she returned rather disconsolately.

"Isn't that sickening! The exchange say the line's out of order; they can't get on."

"Nonsense," said Alan. "Why should it be? I suppose Helen just hasn't heard the telephone."

"No," answered Glenda. "The man says it's something wrong with the line at 'The Towers.' There's nothing wrong with the line to London, and it isn't that Helen doesn't answer. He says he can't make any connexion. He's reporting it, but he doesn't suppose we'll get through before to-morrow morning."

"Oh, well," said Alan. "It doesn't really matter, of course. As you didn't get through, you needn't put it on the pad, and Daddy won't try and get on himself when he comes in now; it's too late." He glanced at the clock, where the time showed itself to be nearly midnight. "Can't think why he isn't back, but we won't wait up for him. He'll lock up when he comes in."

They went off to bed, and to Diana, who fell asleep very promptly, it seemed nearly dawn when she was roused by a faint sound outside her door. Startled at first, she soon realized it was only the noise made by some one shooting the bolts of the front door and, remembering it must be her host returned home, she turned over and settled down again without bothering even to turn on her light and see what the hour really was. 'How late he is; must be about two o'clock,' she thought drowsily, as she dropped off again.

Indeed she was slightly amused to think how mistaken she had been in her ideas of time when the subject came up at breakfast next day.

"How late were you last night, Daddy?" asked Glenda just as the meal came to an end and John Murray was preparing to get up from the table.

"Oh! about half-past twelve, I think," he answered. "I went out for a run. I felt I wanted to clear some worries out of my mind.

I was a bit later than I'd meant to be as I took a wrong turning in the mist. Why, did I disturb you? Sorry if I did."

"Oh! no, I didn't mean that, but Mr. Penrose wanted you to ring up when you came in, and I forgot to leave the message for you on the hall-table. But you'd have been too late anyway, I expect."

"Did you by any chance think of getting on to Helen?" asked her father. "I didn't do it before I went out, and I don't suppose you thought of it?"

"Yes, I did, but their line was out of order," and she recounted the failure of the night before.

"Oh, well," replied John. "It doesn't really matter. I just felt Helen a bit on my conscience last night. Perhaps I'll try and get on after I've done with old Penrose."

The exchange, however, when tackled later in the morning, replied that the line was still out of order, and John Murray, feeling that further efforts were not necessary and that Helen would herself ring them up if she wanted to do so, once the line was cleared, went off to negotiate his purchase of land and decided to leave the occupants of "The Towers" to their own devices.

Chapter III

THE BODY

"By violent hands took off her life"

Macbeth.

Two days later Alan Murray went up the steep flight of steps leading to the front door of "The Towers." It was about five o'clock, but he had left the office early as his head had been aching badly. It was still, of course, broad daylight, and Alan noticed with surprise that the yellow rays of the setting sun were striking across the drawn buff blinds of Helen Bailey's rooms. Helen had a corner sitting-room, looking on to the gardens on one side, and on the drive on the other. Her own separate bathroom and bedroom were the rooms over the porch and hall. Thus three of the big windows facing Alan as he went up the steps were those of Helen's rooms, and he wondered immediately why they should be already shut up in this wholly unaccustomed way. He put his key into the latch, but found to his annoyance that the door was on the chain. Remembering his grandfather's particular ways when the house was empty or maids out, he knocked and rang, but was equally surprised and disgusted when his grandfather in person took off the chain, flung open the door, and without a word of greeting returned to the study from whence he had issued. Alan realized immediately that there was thunder in the air. However, nothing could be done to avoid an interview, and he stepped into the house, to be struck at once with the complete silence and emptiness which seemed to greet him, until he recollected that the three younger maids were still in the country and the cook away with her broken arm. Presumably Helen had not yet found a satisfactory temporary. Hanging up his hat, he turned into the study to the right of the front door. There sat his grandfather by the side of a rather untidy hearth, which again caught Alan's eye by its unwonted aspect.

"Good evening, Grandfather, how are you?" he began, and then, again uneasily conscious of something slightly peculiar in the atmosphere, "Where is Helen? Is anything wrong?"

"Wrong," replied his grandfather, turning on him with a positively baleful glare of his blue eyes. "Wrong, I should think there is!" And with an angry snort returned fiercely to his evening newspaper. Then, as if unable to keep silence, flung it down and broke out: "Wrong! why, what do you think I've had to put up with over the week-end? Look after myself, and have my meals at restaurants." Then, as Alan stood amazed at this totally unexpected statement, the old man went on, "Helen went off somewhere on the Friday night, heavens knows why or when; left me alone, and she's not come back yet."

"Helen went off?" repeated Alan incredulously. "But she couldn't—she'd never do such a thing."

"She could and she did," snapped old James fiercely, but before Alan could collect himself the sound of a key clicking in the latch heralded his father's arrival, and he thankfully went out into the hall to tell him the astounding news. To his surprise John Murray's face grew perceptibly grave and he hurried into the study.

"What's this, Father?" he began, with none of his usual rather nervous deference. "Helen gone and you left alone in the house?"

"Yes, indeed," came stormily from old James, now standing and glaring angrily from the hearth-rug. "I tell you she's been gone the whole week-end and I've had neither sight nor sound of her. I went out for a walk on Friday afternoon as the weather cleared towards four o'clock, and I wanted some fresh air. I met Roger Halliday and went in for a cup of tea with him, and stayed talking and didn't get back till after seven. I found no lights, and the house empty, and just this wild scrawl on the hall-table." Turning to the mantelpiece he took from it a rather crumpled half sheet of paper. Across it was scribbled almost illegibly "Obliged to go away—please go to your club" and an initial which might have been "H." but was too shakily written to be anything very clear.

John Murray stood gazing at the scrap of paper as if it had bitten him, while his father continued in the same fierce and threatening tones, "My club! and well she knew it was closed while they put in that new staircase! and she knew perfectly well that I never will set foot in the other great caravanserai—I can't think how she came to suggest such a thing!"

"But, Father," broke in John, "this isn't Helen's writing, it's not from her this note—surely something is wrong." He turned towards the stairs, for he, too, had noticed that row of windows with blank blinds staring at the sun. His father interrupted in turn, "I suppose something *is* wrong, but anyway Helen's not in the house. I went up to her room directly I found the note, but her doors are all locked and were locked then, and no key to be found to open them."

"Locked!" exclaimed both John and young Alan, and glanced amazed at each other. "Why, Father," resumed John, "this is odder than ever. Why on earth should Helen lock up her rooms?"

"I suppose because she knew there were no maids in the house," replied old James stiffly, "and that 'daily' only came for an hour or two yesterday to sweep and make my bed. Perhaps Helen didn't like the idea of leaving her rooms open in an empty house, but I can't say what she thought—" His proffered explanation sounded singularly unconvincing to John and Alan, knowing Helen's calm indifference to those around her. Besides, who would lock a whole set of rooms and go off taking the key, go off, too, with so little warning and leaving no better word of explanation to an employer of nearly twelve years' standing? And would Helen—Helen the efficient and considerate—ever leave the dreaded and respected Mr. James Murray to the mercies of a "daily"? No, there was more than appeared in this. "And besides," thought John, as he began hurriedly to mount the stairs, "that note isn't Helen's writing, and Father knows it isn't."

At the head of the stairs he paused, and looking over his shoulder at his father, said:

"Are there no keys left in *any* of the locks?"

"Of course not, or I should have used them," replied James angrily. "What do you take me for?"

"And you've been here these three days, with Helen disappeared and the rooms locked, and got no one in to undo the doors?" John sounded more and more perturbed.

"No, indeed," replied James furiously. "If she chose to go off like that and leave her rooms locked up, they'd stay locked till she came back, as far as I cared. I wasn't going to put myself out as to what she was up to."

Again John and Alan glanced at each other, both thoroughly uneasy and horrified at this extraordinary situation. Neither could conceive how Helen could have gone off in this manner; both felt that some clue lay in the locked rooms, and both in their hearts thought James' behaviour as extraordinary in its way as Helen's.

"You should have telephoned to us, Father," said John quietly, "and either you could have joined us or Glenda would have come up to look after you."

"Nothing of the sort," retorted James, still furiously angry. "We'd had enough fuss and commotion over your week-end as it was. I expected Helen back any minute, and I knew in any case that you and Alan would be back this evening. I couldn't go off and leave the house with no one in it at all."

The three men stood now on the landing, gazing at the row of closed doors which faced them, strong handsome mahogany doors, for this was the main part of the first floor, and the rooms had been those meant for the lady of the house. Alan broke the silence:

"The spare-room key might fit," pointing to a door at the end of the corridor—"all these doors are alike."

"I never thought of that," exclaimed old James, and pushing past his son and grandson, he hurried to the door at the end of the corridor on the right, opened it, and took out the key which had been on the inside.

Returning, he pushed it into the lock of the door on the extreme left, that of Helen's sitting-room, a moment's pause, then a faint click: the key fitted, James turned the handle and opened the door and the three went in.

The landing outside was full of bright evening light coming in from the big window that faced the head of the stairs. The room they entered seemed in comparison very dark at first, for the blind was down. While Alan stepped across and hurriedly pulled it up, the two older men looked round. All seemed in order, until John, looking at the carpet, exclaimed, "Why, the carpet's wet!" Alan looked hastily down, to see, as a broad beam of sun fell across the floor, that the carpet did indeed look damp, as if it had been washed, he thought. Moved by the same impulse, all went towards the door leading to the bathroom. That room, too, was empty and seemed as usual. With an instinctive feeling of strain, Alan found himself hanging back instead of going towards the bedroom which lay beyond and into which his father and grandfather had already disappeared. A loud inarticulate exclamation made him spring forward, but at the same moment his father rushed out and pushed him back crying: "Good God, Alan, she's here—she's murdered!" Then, collecting his energies and pulling himself together, he turned back and with Alan went once more into the bedroom, where James, the calmest of the three, was pulling up the blinds of each of the large windows in turn and letting in a flood of evening light.

At the first glimpse there seemed nothing wrong. The furniture was all in place; nothing was overturned or disarranged. The bed, which blocked up half the available floor space, was a real Victorian half-tester, made of heavy walnut, with a high footboard, and a solid back reaching nearly to the ceiling. From the tester, green and red curtains in old chintz hung to the floor. It looked as if it had been slept in, for the bedclothes were rumpled and the eiderdown hung partly over the side. But no one lay in it, and indeed the room seemed empty and deserted. Moving further into the room and past the foot of the bed, it became clear that the room was not empty. Something came into view. For, by the side of the bed, partially screened by its curtains, lying face downwards, was the practically naked body of a woman. The legs and trunk were stretched out towards the far corner of the room, the head and neck, which were lying towards the foot of the bed, were hidden from sight by some white garment, wrapped in a huddled way as it seemed around them. Her arms stuck stiffly out from this white confusion. Her hands, protruding towards the three men, showed in the sunlight that they were terribly mangled, and there were deep cuts and slashes on the arms as well. John Murray knelt down, his father and Alan standing motionless. None of them spoke. John put his hand shrinkingly on the bare white back and drew it away hastily. "Stone cold!" No one said a word. Those long slender limbs, and that well-formed body, they knew were Helen's. Yet, as if impelled by some absolute necessity to know, without possibility of doubt, John, in spite of fingers that shook, untwisted the confusion of lace and silk, and, with some difficulty, turned the body over. A vague croak of horror came from old James at the appalling sight. For, though the body itself, apart from the hands, had shown no signs of violence, the state of the face and head were ghastly. A great gaping cut ran from the forehead across the nose, which was practically cut in two, down to the left cheek. Further gashes on the sides of the head had bled profusely and clotted in great dark masses. One ear was almost off, and as John let fall the dreadful unrecognizable face, it dropped back in a way which showed yet further deep cuts and slashes all around the back of the neck and ears. Only the dark hair, still plaited in 'shells' on each side seemed to recall in any way the woman they had known, and the climax of horror lay in the very incongruity between those still shining plaits and the disfigured travesty of a face.

John Murray could scarcely speak, but from his dry throat he managed to force a few hoarse words, "Come on, we can do nothing. We must fetch the police." He rose unsteadily to his feet and all three passed stumblingly back through the empty rooms, and Alan, despatched by John, fled thankfully down the drive to summon the doctor, who lived near by, while John himself tried to control his shaking hands and lips as he telephoned to the police station. Old James, meanwhile, stood gloomily impassive by the untidy ash-strewn hearth in the study, and, as Alan's unwilling legs brought him back into the house, accompanied by Dr. Graham, he heard his grandfather exclaim in a tone in which a sort of angry exaltation seemed to mix with irritation, "To think she's been lying here all the time while I've been wondering what in God's name she was up to!"

Dr. Graham was the practitioner who attended the Murray family. He knew them all well, and it was he who had been called in by Helen Bailey only the previous Friday to set Mrs. Randall's arm. He could hardly credit the summons brought him by the almost fainting Alan. "Helen's been murdered! Father wants you to come round at once." A few brief questions brought him little enlightenment, for any efforts to explain only brought before Alan's eyes the horrible vision of what he had seen in that bedroom. The doctor realized he was only wasting time, and, hurriedly snatching up his case, rushed to "The Towers." There old James met him with grim self-possession, and, himself turning back into the study, bade the doctor go upstairs. "There's nothing for you to do, but I suppose you'd better go and have a look at her. The police should be here directly." Then, noticing Alan's ashy face, "You'd do more good attending to this weak-nerved fellow here," he added contemptuously.

Dr. Graham, however, felt more inclined to sympathize with Alan's collapse than with the old man's calm, when he in turn knelt by the body and noted the terribly mangled state of what had been the face and neck. He could not but think with repulsion of James Murray spending the week-end alone in that house, concerning himself so little whether all was well in those closed rooms, sleeping and eating with that corpse lying there undiscovered.

He saw, of course, at once that there was nothing whatever for him to do, and that everything had better be left untouched until the arrival of the police. John Murray had stood silently beside him while he made a cursory examination. Glancing up at him, Dr. Graham could only say briefly that death had taken place many hours previously and that, of course, there could be no question of suicide. This was a clear case of murder. Getting to his feet, he in turn looked round the room. It was growing dusk and nothing was to be specially noted in the dimness. Passing back into the sitting room, the light from the landing was falling full across the floor, and he too, noticing its appearance, stooped and laid his fingers upon it, feeling the surface. But as he went down the stairs the roar of a big fast car coming up the hill and sweeping in along the drive signalled the arrival of the police. Merely stopping to give his name and address and say a few brief words to the police surgeon, he went back to his own house and proceeded to note briefly in his private diary what he had himself seen at "The Towers," for he foresaw that this was likely to be a case which would attract a great deal of attention.

For the next few hours the formerly quiet and sedate mansion became the scene of furious activity.

Chapter IV

THE POLICE

"Most probable that so she died"

Antony and Cleopatra.

The organization of the police has shared in the general development of modern life. Here, as elsewhere, the services of an expert class are now available in a big city. Thus, when John Murray telephoned to the Highstead police station, he set in motion an elaborate piece of machinery. The reserve man at the station operated the telephone, and he at once put the call through to the Station Officer. In the case of Highstead, this was an inspector. He, in turn, immediately notified the Superintendent in charge of the Division, the Divisional Surgeon, and the Detective-Inspector attached to the Division, for a London police station has attached to it a small corps of regular C.I.D. men.

The detective-inspector would be the officer appointed to conduct the inquiry. He would do all the work, aided by a detective-sergeant and two or three ordinary detectives, these all being C.I.D. men. Highstead had attached to its police station an exceptional officer in Detective-Inspector Woods. He was a man of about 36, not at all resembling the stolid matter-of-fact man of routine. He was highly intelligent, and of the imaginative, introspective type, widely read and taking an interest in such subjects as psychology and the latest theories of mental development. This was to have its effect on the history of the Murray case. In appearance he was tall, thin, and dark, with blue eyes. One would have taken him perhaps for a lawyer or a writer, not for a detective. He was a man who was very susceptible to impressions, always keen to get beneath appearances to the character of the persons with whom he was brought in contact. He believed a good deal in the wisdom embodied in the saying "A man is known by the company he keeps". In other words, he did attach importance to the general belief in an individual held by friends and intimates. Sometimes facts could be, and were, distorted, but an estimate of character formed after years of close knowledge was, he held, usually reliable. This led him often to keep his judgment in suspense, and to work patiently and tenaciously away at cases which others would consider closed. The chance that a man of this temperament was now placed in charge of the murder at "The Towers" proved of the greatest importance, for that case was to develop along lines in which correct judgment of the characters of the persons involved was essential.

The first instructions given to John Murray on the telephone were naturally that he was to see that nothing in the room where the murder had been discovered was moved, that the body should be left untouched, and that nobody should be allowed to leave the house. Then, stopping to pick up the Divisional Surgeon, and followed by Detective-Sergeant Riley, Detectives Brown and Wilson, and by men with the finger-print and flashlight apparatus, Woods set off for "The Towers." Scotland Yard would automatically take over the case, as it came within the London area. A superintendent from the Yard would be put in charge, but Inspector Woods, working under his supervision, would remain the officer actually carrying out the investigation, and, as such, he proceeded at once to the scene of the crime.

On entering "The Towers," he first briefly interviewed the head of the household, who met him in the hall. He noted the names of the family, the fact that James Murray had been alone in the house during the week-end, but that the discovery of the crime had not been made until this very evening, indeed only an hour before. The identity of the body was spoken to by both James and John, and the note found by James on the Friday was handed to him. He was told that the doors upstairs had been, and still remained, locked, with the exception of the door of the sitting-room, opened by another key. He asked if any search had been made for the actual key belonging to the room, but was told that nothing had been done. Indeed, beyond finding that the body was that of Helen Bailey, and calling in the doctor to corroborate what was obvious, that she was dead, nothing had been attempted. Satisfied that he would find the scene of the crime untouched, the Inspector prepared to investigate it. John Murray, shepherding the Inspector, was obliged to return to the bedroom to explain the position of the body when first seen and how he had moved it.

"Lying on her face, was she?" murmured the Inspector, busily writing in his note-book. "Legs extended towards the head of the bed, arms stretched stiffly out away from the trunk and upwards towards the head."

"This,—I think it is her vest, Inspector—was pulled up and twisted about her face and neck. I had to disentangle it when I looked to see who it was," John Murray gulped, as he saw again that mangled mass which, of itself, could scarcely tell him whose face it had been.

"Hum! Looks to me like this," said the Inspector, turning to the sergeant, and to the surgeon who was now in his turn bending over the corpse. "See here, Riley, the body has been dragged in here," and he pointed to a messy trail, not plain blood but a vague wide stain reaching from the door to where the body lay. "Dragged by the feet, I'd say, with the head and arms trailing on the ground, and the vest in that way worked up round the face. Then, when he'd got the trunk and head round here out of sight of the door, he twisted the legs and feet to get them alongside into this narrow space beside the bed. That accounts for the way the arms lie, and for the vest being pulled up and tangled round the neck and head. It implies, too, that only one person did this, and that some one with no very great physical strength, who was obliged to drag the body as best he could." The surgeon and the sergeant nodded agreement. The body was laid again on its face, as it had been when found. Its actual position had not been shifted, and the flashlight photographs were soon taken. Then, under the supervision of the divisional surgeon, it was removed to the mortuary, and the police began the task of examining the house.

At once various things began to come to light. "Look here, sir," said Sergeant Riley, holding up a crumpled ball of bloodstained linen. "Poked away under the washstand," he said briefly. Spread out, it proved to be a sheet, deeply stained and stiffened with blood. "Basin emptied and wiped out, nothing there. May have finger-prints, of course." Then turning to the bed, he flung back the eiderdown and blankets. There was no top sheet, and the lower sheet, still in place, was only spotted, not deeply stained. The pillow was not in place on the bolster, but had been pushed down into the bed. It was widely, but not darkly, patched, and was much crumpled. "Why," remarked Woods, stooping to examine it closely, "this has had water on it: looks almost as if it had been washed," and indeed the spots and marks had clearly been diluted and partially obliterated with water. The blankets, too, gave a peculiar indication. They appeared to have been taken off the bed, for the under one was slightly stained on its lower surface, but the marks did not correspond with those on the lower sheet, while the upper one had spots and streaks resembling ash-smears. Neither was at all badly marked, unlike the sheet, and it was clear the sheet had been taken off and used to mop up a large quantity of blood.

"And see here, sir," said Brown, who had been examining the walls and windows, and who now pointed to the back of the door leading to the sitting-room. On its gleaming white painted surface, about fourteen inches from the ground, ran a conspicuous horizontal line, again clearly a bloodstain.

"Let's have more light, Riley," said the Inspector, and as the switches clicked down, lights sprang up on the dressing-table, the bedside-table, and from the old-fashioned cluster-of-three hanging from the centre of the ceiling. The bedside light cast its rather bright beams down on to the patch of floor lying between the bed and the washstand. Before the washstand lay a fairly large mat, of that pale cream Japanese matting much favoured by housewives of former days. "Look at *this*" said the Inspector loudly. The other two moved round, and all three stood staring. Clearly shown up by the electric light, outlined on the plain matting, were the prints of a naked foot. "Blood, that is, too," added Inspector Woods, and so it undoubtedly was. "Well, if we've not got finger-prints, we've got footprints, and I suppose they're as individual as the others and a lot more unusual in this medium." "Small prints," observed Sergeant Riley in his turn, bending closer—"a woman's, but not *hers*—not the dead one's, she'd long narrow feet, on the big side, I'd say. These are smaller and squarer." "Prints are smaller than the feet themselves," remarked Woods. "Yes, but not so much smaller, and I'd swear these are broader than the dead woman's and stumpier, so to speak, but they'll need to be measured, and her feet as well, very carefully too, after this."

"Don't let the Press get wind of these prints," said the Inspector. "We'll keep them to ourselves until we know a bit more about them. They may yet turn out to be Miss Bailey's."

Swiftly the search went on. Drawers and cupboards were opened and their contents carefully checked. One drawer of the dressing-table had a special lock, but the key was in it, and the drawer itself was empty. There were a few spots and smears which looked like blood on the white paper with which it was lined. "She'd very nice things," mused the Inspector, as he rapidly opened the other drawers, refolded garments and put them back in the place they had come from. "Spent a good deal on herself, I'd say. Judging by her clothes, I'd expect her to have some good jewellery—ought to be about—but no sign so far. We must wait to get hold of some member of the household. Ask Mr. Murray to send for his granddaughter to come up to town. She'll be able to tell us what's missing, for there is a good deal missing I'll be bound, and we don't want to lose time."

"A good deal missing," replied Riley, "and to my mind too much present."

"What do you mean by that?" queried Woods.

"Too many marks, and too much blood," said Riley. "Doesn't seem sensible to me, wiping things up with that sheet, tidying the bed, and then leaving footprints in blood on the mat, stains on the door, and that spotted paper in the drawer, and Wilson here says there are more prints in the sitting-room."

"Well, we've about finished in here. Send in the finger-print men and let them go over everything," said the Inspector, satisfied that everything had been thoroughly gone over. "We'll have to take that mat along, of course, and, Riley, just measure the height of that smear on the door, and tell them to take a flashlight of it carefully."

They moved on into the bathroom. It was only a very small slip-room, with an old-fashioned fitted bath but with no fixed washbasin, hence the presence of the washstand in the bedroom. Here everything was in order—the floor, covered with linoleum, was clean and dry. There were no soiled towels or any signs of anything unusual.

"No marks found here, sir," said Riley. "No prints on the taps, or even on the door-handles. We've tested it all very thoroughly and I can't find any sort of traces. The only thing is the sponge; it must, I think, have been used; it's rather discoloured, but has been well rinsed and soaked. I'm afraid it's no real help to us."

The remaining room was the sitting-room. Here there were no apparent signs of disorder. The heavy old-fashioned furniture was all in place, the big armchair drawn up by the fireplace had been sat in, the cushions were indented, but the smaller chairs and the sofa showed no signs of having been used.

"She'd been here alone," mused Woods. "She'd sat in this chair herself evidently, but the one opposite hasn't been drawn up to the fire, and the sofa cushions are all neat as the maid would leave them. Fire been lit, I see." He knelt down and looked at the hearth. There was a good deal of ash heaped up and cinders. "Must have had this burning a good many hours," he remarked. He glanced into the scuttle, which was quite empty. "Find out from the maids if this scuttle had been full on the Friday morning, and, if so, have the fire lit, and time how long it takes to burn a scuttle. And sieve the ashes, of course."

Seeing Riley looked puzzled, he went on to explain. "There's been a fire here, I should say, judging from the amount of ash and cinder, for seven or eight hours. Now that's a good length of time in the summer. Even if the weather is wet and cold, one wouldn't expect this sitting-room fire to be going all day. More probably she lit it in the evening, when it grew chillier. We must find out for certain, of course, if any of the household know whether it had been lit in the morning before they left the house. But my belief is this was lit towards evening, and, if so, it was burning pretty well all night, and we'll have to try and find out what bearing that has on the events that took place in this room."

Riley had been listening attentively. "Well," he said, "another thing, sir, if you're right, and this fire was burning most of the night, it makes me wonder why this floor is still a bit damp."

"Damp!" exclaimed Woods.

"Why, yes, sir; you see it's been very thoroughly washed over. You can see discolourations and stains all over it, especially here near the hearth, but they've been well scrubbed. If it had been a dark carpet they'd pretty well have been obliterated. Now a good fire burning for hours would help considerably to dry the damp, yet, if you feel it, you'll tell for yourself, it's still pretty wet."

Woods stooped and passed his hands over the surface. "Yes, it is a little damp, as you say. But it's a thick carpet, Riley; it might take two days to dry thoroughly."

Both remained thoughtful for a moment. Then Woods resumed, "Well, make the tests I've spoken of as soon as you can. Now, what else can we find?" They began to examine walls and furniture with care, and soon other discoveries came to light. To the right of the fireplace, low down near the floor, were streaks of blood, like the blurred impressions of a hand. They seemed to have been made by some one putting their hand on the wall and drawing it downwards. Woods made a careful note, and directed that a photograph should be taken and the piece of wall itself covered up for the present.

Then, in a tall built-in cupboard which filled the recess to the left of the fireplace, further most peculiar stains were found. The woodwork of the room was dark green, but the inside of the cupboard door was a paler shade. The cupboard had contained shelves, which had been removed, and it was quite empty. High up, right along the top piece of the door on the inside, were perfectly distinct dark smears. Woods was a tall man, and stepping forward he put his hand up and fitted his fingers to the marks. Clearly they must have been made by some one of a fair height, a small person could barely have reached.

"How tall do you think Miss Bailey is?" he enquired of Riley.

"About five feet seven or eight, I should say," replied Riley.

"H'm—she might have made these," said Woods thoughtfully. "Have the height of this door noted carefully, please, Riley," and again he fitted his own fingers in. Then, stepping into the cupboard, he tried to see if he could close the door behind him and found that, as there was no handle on the inside, this was not very easy. "Well," he said, emerging, "all we can say for certain is that some one, with cut or stained hands, was in this cupboard. We'll have these stains photographed and enlarged, but I'm afraid we'll not get much from them, either, in the way of identification. It'll be difficult to get a print from the dead woman's hands, they're so slashed about."

Search of the bureau produced nothing. Neatly kept household accounts, papers in beautiful order, no sign of anything missing or disarranged. A small metal box, locked, was marked petty cash, but, as it showed when rattled about, money was still in it.

"We must find her keys," said Woods, "and make sure what money is here, and try to find out if she'd much cash in this room. But I don't think plain robbery is the motive here, or we'd find drawers taken out and everything thrown about. Either the murderer knew where anything he or she wanted was kept—or they've tidied up uncommonly well. It's the greatest drawback so much time has elapsed since the murder was done."

At length everything that could be examined had been carefully gone over, all possible places tested for prints, the taking of photographs was finished, and dawn was breaking as Woods, his task for the present completed, drove wearily home to snatch a few hours' rest. He felt in a curious state. No one can view a battered corpse, or inspect the scene of a bloody crime, without some tingling of the nerves. Woods felt this was a strange case, and already it seemed to him an unpleasant one. He agreed with Riley's criticism—there were too many stains and clues—and a feeling of anxiety and depression came over him. He was afraid lest he might have missed something, and still more afraid he had not read the signs aright. Above all, being a very decent fellow, he thought with great distaste of the ghoulish outburst in which the daily Press was sure to indulge. Then, realizing he had been officially put in charge of this case and must not let his nerves and feelings affect him, he tried to dismiss it from his thoughts, with the sensible resolve to wait till morning brought its fresh inspirations.

Chapter V

THE PROBLEM

"He'll then instruct us of this body"

Cymbeline.

The next afternoon C.I.D. Superintendent Gowing sat in his office gazing at the already quite imposing mass of notes which Inspector Woods had laid before him.

"It's a queer case, sir," said the Inspector, "or rather," correcting himself, "there seem to be some funny twists in it."

"Well," said the Superintendent, "go ahead," and the Inspector began:

"First of all, the medical side, sir. The report's here. There are two sets of wounds. One, the big blow across the forehead. The doctor thinks she, Miss Bailey, was either standing or sitting when that was struck. If she were standing, then the blow was struck by some one taller than herself, say a person of close on six feet, for it clearly came from above downwards. It was done by a right-handed person, with a fair amount of force behind it. The person was facing her and must himself have been standing up. If she were sitting, then the blow might have been struck by a much smaller person, for, in that way, we should get the same effect of the blow coming from a point above her head. More than that, the doctor can't say.

"It was a very severe injury, and must have rendered her unconscious. She had bled very profusely for some time, as the edges of the wound show. The doctors think that this wound would not have proved fatal, for no vital injury was done. But in order to save her, she needed prompt medical attention, which, of course, she did not get. She might have regained consciousness. In any case, the further injuries were inflicted at a later period, but when she was still alive.

"The second set of injuries were inflicted from behind, while Miss Bailey was lying on the ground on her face. They are mostly on the left side of the neck and head. One very deep, bad wound cut right down into the throat; another practically cut off the ear; all that side of the neck and back of the head pretty well mangled, fourteen different wounds, three others on the right hand side. None of the blows show very great force. Dr. James and Dr. Graham agree they were done by some one with no particular strength, either by a woman or by an old man." He paused, significantly, but the Superintendent said nothing. Woods went on: "The face and chest had been washed, after the first attack, before the second; not, of course, by Miss Bailey herself—she'd have been pretty well unconscious after that first blow, and too blinded by the blood to find her way to a basin, much less to bathe herself thoroughly."

"You mean the murderer washed her?" queried the Superintendent incredulously.

"Don't know about that, sir, but washed she had been, and carefully, and the wound on the forehead bathed thoroughly. The vest too was still slightly damp where the blood had at one time been washed from her neck."

"Poor woman," murmured the Superintendent, visualizing against his will some one bathing those wounds with the grim knowledge that far worse and more brutal ones were to be inflicted.

"I think," went on Woods, "that the first attack was made in the bedroom. She'd most naturally be there undressing, and she undressed before this happened, for her underclothes were neatly folded, with no stains or spots whatever, on the chair the other side of the bed. Then, though the bigger stains and marks had been fairly thoroughly washed off the floor, there were a few big splashes, towards the fireplace, which, from their shape, show they'd been thrown outwards from a centre near the dressing-table. The doctors say if her body fell there, after the first blow, those splashes are just what they'd expect to find. But I'll come back to that point later, when I come to the second attack."

The Superintendent nodded his agreement.

"We'll assume then that she was in her bedroom, undressed at some time about six o'clock, when the first attack was made, and she was struck down unconscious. I've verified that she was in the habit of having a bath before dinner, so that fits in. She didn't of course die as early as that, but we can't fix the time of death; it was too long before the body was found."

Again Gowing signified that he followed the argument.

"Then," resumed the Inspector briskly, "the state of the bed showed she'd been in the bed, probably with those first injuries, and the pillow had been stained, but water had splashed pretty freely *over* the stains, almost washed them out in places. Some one had tried later to clean up, the floor had been sponged over pretty thoroughly, the basin had been wiped out with that sheet. There were no finger-prints anywhere. But, what seems so extraordinary, that mat with the bloody footprints hadn't been touched. I can't quite understand it. Those prints, specially one of the right foot, are as clear and distinct as anything I've ever seen. Whoever cleaned up hadn't touched them. Possibly they saw they'd be difficult to obliterate, but the rug, which was only light matting really, could easily be taken away and burned, and they probably meant to do this but were interrupted before they'd done so. Mr. Murray came back after dark, and came slowly up the drive. That room faces the drive, and the murderer may have heard him coming and made off. There's some possible confirmation of that in the next room."

Woods paused, but the Superintendent remained silent, automatically jabbing his pencil on the paper before him, for his mind too was considering the immense possibilities and the great importance of the footprints.

Seeing that Gowing did not intend to give an inkling of his thoughts, Woods went on: "Then, the other two rooms—the bathroom floor had been washed, must have been, that's to say, for it was dry and didn't show, but the trail of blood in the bedroom ran from the body right to the communicating door, and must have gone through. Indeed," he went on, very seriously, "I'm pretty well satisfied, Superintendent, that the actual murder was done in the sitting-room, that's to say the final attack was made there, which proved fatal."

"But the bloodstains in the bed?" objected the Superintendent.

"Well, sir, it's like this. The sitting-room was stained here and there and everywhere, though it had been pretty well washed, too. The carpet there was a pale buff, and the stains wouldn't wash out so thoroughly and showed more. There's a great deal of staining before the fireplace. The fire had been lit, I've ascertained, some time during the late afternoon or evening of Friday, it being a cold, wet, dreary day. Then there were some small stains on the wall to the right of the fire, marks like a bleeding hand drawn downwards, and the hands of the corpse were badly mangled in the second attack."

"How do you deduce that's the mark of her hand?"

"The doctors say she was lying down when the second lot of blows were struck. She must have been struck first on one side—the left—and she then tried to roll away and put up her hands to save her head. She then flung her hands out and touched the wall. The marks are right down on the little piece of wall beside the fireplace near the ground, and they're marks of a hand drawn downwards towards the floor. The murderer would be standing over her, and he, or she, would draw his hands *upwards*, supposing they were stained too."

The Superintendent nodded to show he agreed with this reasoning.

"Then there's a most peculiar staining in a big cupboard that stands in the corner of the room. It's a big, built-in thing, empty, for it was to be fitted with shelves and had been cleared in readiness. The stains are high up, inside, right at the top of the door—finger-marks, but too blurred for print identification. They're the murderer's marks too," he added angrily, "showing he hid in there and held the door shut. There's no handle inside. I've tried it myself, and I'm sure that's how those marks were made."

"That means he—or she—was hiding from some one, some third person," said the Superintendent, with a gleam in his eye—"some one who went into that room, after the murder and before those doors were locked—went in and went out, and saw nothing perhaps? Could that have happened?"

"Possibly, but there's another alternative. It's possible that the murderer heard Mr. Murray return, heard him come up the drive and let himself into the house. The murderer then locked the sitting-room door hurriedly but hadn't time to get to the bathroom and bedroom doors, so dashed into the cupboard for cover. Actually the other two doors were locked on the inside, the keys are in them still, but he—or she—might not know that. The finger-prints on the keys show that Miss Bailey had locked those other two doors herself. There are some blurred marks on the bedroom key, but the only clear ones are Miss Bailey's."

"What about the sitting-room key?"

"Nowhere to be found, the door had been locked and the key taken away. We've searched the place most carefully, but it's not to be found. And that brings us to the other point connected with that, one of the most puzzling things about the whole case."

"One moment, Inspector," interrupted Gowing. "I suppose you've questioned Mr. Murray very carefully about his own movements? Did he hear nothing whatever when he came in? After all, he was the person who might have alarmed the murderer."

Woods answered emphatically, "Well, sir, I've put him through it as thoroughly as it's possible to do. He was, of course, he said, willing and ready enough to answer questions. He was out with his friend, as he says. I've had that checked, and he must have got home at the time he says, too, seven o'clock. I've verified that by the hour he left his friend's house. He declares he found that note in the front hall, that he went up at once to Miss Bailey's room, and found all the doors locked, and not a sound to be heard anywhere. He noticed her blinds were down, but it was getting dusk and that didn't surprise him. That he sticks to. Of course he behaved strangely, in one sense, in making no effort to open the doors and in not communicating with the family, but he says he expected her to return at any time, and never dreamt of breaking open her rooms once she'd locked them. Anyway, we can't get any more out of him, and of course his behaviour may be quite normal and correct. I haven't been able to find anything against him at all."

"Very well," said Gowing. "Now what else were you going to tell me? Something about the keys, weren't you?"

"There's no doubt that the murderer locked that sitting-room door and took the key away. But the question then arises, how did the murderer ever get into the house, and into those rooms? It's like this: I find, on questioning the household, that Mr. Murray was always extremely strict and particular about the house being locked up. He wouldn't for years have anything but a chain to the front door and an ordinary handle. He only agreed to a Yale lock being put on a few months ago, when Mr. John Murray made a great point of it. Even then he only had keys made to fit for himself, Mr. John and Mr. Alan. He absolutely forbade either Miss Bailey or Miss Glenda to have one. He laid it down too that Mr. Alan was to keep his key on his watch-chain and not lend it to his sister or any one. In fact, there was a great deal of fuss and a good deal of disagreeableness over the keys. Now, as the household was away and the house to be so empty, all the side and back doors were properly locked and bolted. Mr. Murray was pretty often left in the house with one or two maids and Miss Bailey when the rest of the household were away in the country. He had absolutely fixed rules for this, and, being a determined old gentleman, he saw that his wishes were carried out. The front door would be kept on the chain the whole time. That, all the household agrees, was his rule and one which was strictly carried out. It follows from that that the front door was properly shut and chained after Mr. Murray went out. He says Miss Bailey came and let him out, and he heard her put on the chain behind him. Now she must have opened the door to let some one in. We know a woman was in the house some time, of course, and the inference is that Miss Bailey let her in. Actually Mr. Murray found the door unlocked, and opened it by the handle alone, when he came back at seven. He was prepared to be very angry, but thought Miss Bailey might have gone somewhere in the grounds for a breath of fresh air, as the rain had stopped. Then he found her note, and believed she had left the house, and, of course, been obliged to close the door behind her and leave it, without any chain or fastening. It leaves a loophole for the murderer, who, having got in, could get out at any time, of course, between Mr. Murray's departure and his return."

"You must also allow for the possibility that the murderer was hidden in the house before Mr. Murray went out," said the Superintendent.

"Yes, sir, but the important fact is this. There is one piece of evidence which seems to show the murderer returned to the house again later on."

"Oh! how's that indicated?"

"Dr. Graham noticed—and so did I myself subsequently—that the carpet in the sitting-room was still damp on Monday evening. Now that implies that some person, presumably the murderer, had been in that room later than the Friday night. Otherwise the carpet would have dried before we got there."

The Superintendent reflected a moment.

"How did old Murray get in and out of the house during the three days he was there? He couldn't put up the chain behind him."

"I went into that pretty thoroughly. The daily woman came on Saturday, and he let her in, and instructed her to stay there until he came back, which he did after luncheon. He lunched at his club, and the daily woman left him a cold supper all ready in the dining-room. He's one of those who don't have tea, and he managed all right, he says. The same arrangement was made on Sunday, and on Monday he knew Mr. John Murray and Mr. Alan would be back, and the woman stayed there all day.

"I've had the woman interviewed, and the times she gave checked, and it was all satisfactory and agreed with what Mr. Murray said. I checked it too by the tradespeople and postmen for Saturday and Monday. She opened the door. She'd been a cook, and could do well enough for Mr. Murray in a plain way, but she wasn't engaged to do more than clean, and she never concerned herself with the upstairs rooms at all. She's not bothered herself much, thought Miss Bailey had been sent for by relations probably, in a case of illness. So she just carried on, did what Mr. Murray told her, and neither thought there was anything wrong, nor looked at anything in particular. Says she never even tried to get in those locked rooms, just went about her business downstairs. I believe her too; she's that kind of woman, and she'd have said, when I examined her, if she'd had any suspicions, been only too ready to say she'd thought there was something odd.

"As to Mr. Murray himself, the only other person who was in the house and the only person who was there alone—during the times when the daily woman wasn't there, of course—we've had to consider him and his statement pretty carefully, especially as the murderer must have taken some time in clearing up. Assuming Miss Bailey went to her bath about six o'clock, Mr. Murray returned just after seven. That doesn't leave too much time for the double attack, and the washing of the first wound, and the considerable amount of cleaning which was done.

"I'm fairly sure, too, that the floor *must* have been done over several times, apart from its being still damp on Monday. It had been very much stained, all over the place, and most carefully and thoroughly washed, and deep bloodstains take a lot of washing. I don't believe half an hour would have done."

"It seems to me odd that such pains were taken with the floor, and yet those marks on the wall and in the cupboard were left."

"They were less conspicuous. The ones on the wall were very low down, and the cupboard only showed when the door was opened widely. They might have been overlooked, whereas the marks on the floor were so obvious they'd have been seen by any one entering the room at once."

"Well, if you're right, then you realize, Inspector, you're leading up to the establishment of the theory that some one entered those rooms, and worked away in them, subsequent to Friday night, and most probably as recently as Sunday night or Monday morning. And that points directly to Mr. James Murray, who is the only person known to have been in the house on the Friday night immediately after the murder had been committed. Naturally, that must bring him under suspicion to a certain extent."

"We can't go beyond that, sir, though, for, as I've told you, I can't find any flaw in his story. There's a little more to consider, too. It's possible that there were special reasons, which we can't guess, why those floors had to be so thoroughly washed. Whoever did it may have felt they'd got to get into those rooms at all costs. The fact that the sitting-room key is gone seems to show the guilty persons still have it, and must have taken it with them anyway. If they watched the house and saw when Mr. Murray left each day, they might somehow have got into the house and gone up. There is a way in by the conservatory, which only has an ordinary lock, no bolts, and a spare key, or even a piece of wire might have undone that door. Not very convincing, I know, sir," seeing Gowing's face, "but it is a possibility which I think we should bear in mind. The daily woman was always either in the kitchen or the study, and it would have been possible to dodge her. I've been driven to consider the idea, because the other evidence does seem to let Mr. Murray out, and to show we've some one else to reckon with.

"I mean, of course, the evidence of those footprints. They are a perfectly definite proof that some person, unknown to us at present, was in that room. As a matter of routine, I've had them measured and compared with the feet of the only two persons who actually were in the house at the time. I was sure myself, from my own observations, that they were not the prints of either of those two, and," finished Woods firmly, "the doctors have measured Miss Bailey's feet, and Mr. James Murray's feet, and neither corresponded in the least with the prints made in blood on the mat. Dr. Williams states that they were made by a woman smaller by a couple of inches than Miss Bailey, and probably by a young, athletic woman."

Chapter VI

THE FOOTPRINTS

"Slaying is the word,
It is a deed in fashion"

Julius Cæsar.

"Yes, go on," said Gowing, for he perceived that Woods' pause indicated there was much more to come.

"Of course, it's a large house, and Mr. Murray was out having his meals and so on, and the daily woman didn't go upstairs but stayed in the kitchen and ground floor. It's just barely possible that the murderer didn't ever leave the house, but was hidden there those two days, and went into the rooms to try to hide his traces. But at once we come up against those footprints there. No one with plenty of time could fail to notice them and try to remove them. That's the really puzzling feature, when one considers how much else was done, and that there are no signs of haste otherwise."

"Well," said Gowing, "it's certainly a queer problem, but it doesn't seem to be at all probable that any one could have remained in the house unknown to Mr. Murray all those days."

"Personally," proceeded Woods, "I can't help thinking that the leaving of those footprints was not an oversight."

The Superintendent grunted. "Do you think the *making* of them was?"

"You mean, are they genuine, or are they faked?"

"Well, yes. It seems to me too much of a good thing—'Woman's footprints made in blood'—sounds like an improvement on the *Sign of Four*," and Gowing quoted with a smile the famous remark of Dr. Watson, "'Holmes, a child has done this horrid thing'."

Woods laughed. "Well, as you know, I feel this whole case has too many clues about it, but I've been over and over these prints with the doctors, and they are certain they are genuine prints, made by a living girl. Of course, they are very conspicuous in a good light, but, if any one were tidying that room in a bad light, they *might* have missed them. Perhaps, too, it was all done when the dusk was thickening, and the woman wouldn't dare switch on the lights to show any one was in those rooms. Or, as I've said, she may have intended to remove the mat bodily, just roll it up and take it away, and then been frightened at the last moment, and forgot. I don't see that at present we can do more than be thankful at least they were forgotten, whatever the cause."

"Either that," said the Superintendent, "or they were left *intentionally*." He laid stress on the words, but before Woods could speak went on: "For again you'll realize it's a mystery why any one should make a bare footprint, then put on their shoes and go off leaving these traces. Presumably she did put on her shoes again, women don't go barefoot in London nowadays. In any case, the woman who made those prints has got to be found."

"No woman is known to have gone to 'The Towers' that evening," answered Woods. "We've tried the neighbouring houses, and the postman and tradesmen who might have been about. No one at all was seen. The house next door was empty, only a caretaker. He thought he heard a car at about midnight, but he's very vague, and can't even be sure if it was Friday night or not. So we come back to this—we must go through all the women who knew that house, or knew Miss Bailey intimately, and see if we can get on to any one in that way. I think we must assume it was some one known well or else how could she have admitted them to the house and to her room?"

"The woman needn't necessarily have been in the bedroom, of course," said Gowing. "They might have been talking to one another through the two rooms, as women often do."

"Well, sir, I've had up all the people in the house, and a good deal has come to light, which may help to trace her. There's Miss Glenda Murray, granddaughter of Mr. James Murray, a young lady of eighteen; she was away in the country, left, in fact, on Friday afternoon. I've verified her alibi and it's all satisfactory. Miss Bailey had been her governess. They were evidently on the best of terms, and Miss Glenda has been through her things to see what was there. Now, sir, it transpires there's a lot of jewellery missing, and, besides, a valuable fur coat. Miss Bailey apparently had an elderly admirer, an old gentleman called Scott. He is partly an invalid, and lives at Bournemouth, but Miss Murray can't give us any address. She knew about him from Miss Bailey. Says it was one of those infatuations old gentlemen sometimes get. Miss Bailey, she thinks, never intended to marry him. She doesn't clearly know if he offered marriage, but they corresponded a great deal. Miss Bailey always shut herself up in her sitting-room every afternoon to write to him. It was a regular joke in the family. She used to go to Bournemouth for her holidays, and met him there originally, and usually went to see him once or twice a year."

"Any of his letters found?"

"No—no sign of them. Miss Murray says he suffered from arthritis and couldn't write himself, she thought—couldn't hold a pen. Sometimes typewritten letters came, but Miss Bailey never showed her anything of the sort. What she did show were the presents he sent. For Christmas he'd given her a pair of very handsome diamond ear-rings, and for her birthday in May a diamond and platinum watch. He'd sent her lots of other things too—a pearl necklace—better than anything Miss Murray has, she says. And in that last cold spell in February he'd sent up a really splendid mink coat, with sable collar and cuffs, worth £200 or so, Miss Murray believes. But everything's gone, it's all missing and there's not a trace of it in those rooms."

"Come now," said Gowing cheerfully, "that ought to help us. Whoever took those things won't have destroyed them. Either they'll have tried at once to sell or pawn them, or they'll have concealed them, and with luck any one hard enough up to murder for gain would have tried to reap the reward of their efforts by getting rid of the things before the murder was found. Notify all the pawnbrokers and usual places in case anything was offered to them last Saturday, and give a description to the Press."

"Yes, I see that," replied Woods, "any one would try to dispose of the things quickly, but it was an incredible chance that old Murray did nothing until his son came back on Monday. If he'd gone up and had those doors broken in on Saturday evening—" he broke off and looked searchingly at the Superintendent.

"Mr. Murray's a strange man," replied Gowing, "always been so rich he could go his own way. I understand he was furiously angry at finding the house and himself left like that, and wasn't going to trouble himself over what Miss Bailey was really up to."

"That's what he says," said Woods, "but I don't feel satisfied. It still seems to me unbelievable he should leave those rooms locked—a lady who'd been with them twelve years, who he knew wouldn't be likely to go off and leave him alone—a note he admits wasn't like her writing—no, I think he knows a lot more than he's told us."

"Possibly," returned Gowing. "We'll need to keep an eye on him of course, but I think you'll find he's all right. Anyhow," he went on, "this missing property gives us a motive, I suppose—robbery for gain, in fact."

Woods didn't answer at once. Then he said slowly, "It's partly that which makes me feel there's a lot beneath this surface, sir, and by that I mean I get the impression this is a *prepared* surface. We're meant to look at it, and at what is so plainly presented on it, but not any deeper. If it had been a murder for robbery, for these valuable things, we know well enough the type that goes in for robbery with violence. Here we've got robbery, and a sort of violence, but the medical men say those blows had no great force behind them—they are definite they weren't struck by any powerful person. Nor does that explanation fit in with one of the things that bother me most—the washing of the wounds between the two attacks. No violent person, intent on theft of jewellery, would stop to do that."

"Well, you can go on thinking over that," said Gowing, "but we've got to get busy and see what ordinary routine can do for us. Now I suppose you've searched all the rooms in the house, and the grounds and so on?"

"Of course," answered Woods, rather indignantly. "Been through every room thoroughly. There's no sign of anything wrong anywhere. A very small smear of blood in one of Mr. James Murray's wardrobe drawers, which he accounts for by a baddish cut he's got on one finger. Nothing in that. No stains on his clothes at all."

"I've had all the ashes from the fireplace sifted. They'd no kitchen fire, the household being away for the week-end, did it all by gas, but he'd a fire in his study, and there'd been the fire in Miss Bailey's room. Nothing abnormal in either, no sign of any material having been burnt, no buttons and so on. I've had the grounds gone over most carefully—nothing buried anywhere. The murderer had wiped most things up with that sheet; possibly washed himself in the bathroom and dried on his own handkerchief. He left nothing behind anywhere."

"The telephone had been cut, but I'd say by an amateur."

The Superintendent gazed at him silently.

"Cut through with some sort of clippers, roughly," amplified Woods.

"What for?"

The Inspector shrugged his shoulders. "Can't say. Old Murray found it out of order on Saturday and notified the Post Office, who put it right for him. Again, might be the usual preliminary to a robbery by some one who believed the house to be empty, went in, surprised her, and struck her down."

"That won't do," said Gowing. "If Miss Bailey was in her rooms, running a bath on and so forth, the noise would be perfectly distinct from the porch, where the telephone line goes down to the Post Office main. Whoever cut the telephone line knew the house was occupied all right. It shows premeditation. Now, let's start from this. We've got precious few facts to go on, and a lot of queer things unexplained, but if we peg away following up the traces we've got, I think they'll lead us in a definite direction. We do know for certain that a woman was there; you can't get away from those footprints, nor from the stains in that cupboard. There was a woman involved, that's one positive fact. And I believe this jewellery and these furs will put us on her track. We must go for these missing things first, Inspector."

Chapter VII

THE SUSPECT

"I'll throw thy body in another's room"

Henry VI.

That belief was justified even more promptly than Gowing had hoped. That same afternoon Woods came into his office again full of jubilation.

"The jewellery was sold on Saturday morning, sir, we've had a notification from Smiths of Burlington Street. A lady—we've got her description—went into their place about ten o'clock on Saturday morning, when they were hardly ready for business. She produced a diamond and platinum watch and a pair of ear-rings for sale, filled up the form and gave a false name and address, as it turns out. Smiths thought it a bona fide affair because she seemed such good style, quiet, rather embarrassed. They do a good deal of that sort of thing for high-class customers, and they assure me she was a good type—well-dressed, absolute lady, and all that. Of course, they kept the slip she'd signed, and here it is." He produced a pink printed form with a signature and address written in a clear hand, 'Edna Jefferson,' "and I think, sir, we'll find it's the same person who wrote that note."

"Extraordinary how these people behave," remarked the Superintendent cynically. "She must have realized we'd be after her and after these jewels, and yet she goes and lets us get a description of her appearance and a sample of her writing. And are there any finger-prints?" she queried.

"No, the manager says she never took her gloves off. She'd *that* amount of sense anyway. And actually the description might fit a hundred young women—small, slim, dark hair and eyes, artificial complexion, age might be anything between twenty and thirty-five—they're all too much of an age nowadays for my taste—nothing very unusual, nothing at all outstanding to differentiate her from any one else."

"Still," persisted Gowing, "we know now, and it's another proof, besides those rather fishy footprints, a woman was in that house, and got that jewellery. And, of course, Woods, you realize from the facts about the chain on the door, she must be a woman Miss Bailey knew well?"

"Because she'd not have let in any one she didn't know, being herself alone in that great house?"

"Yes, and more than that," reflected Gowing. "She took her up to her own room. And I tell you, Woods, I'm pretty sure from other points that she was well known to the family, and what we must do now is to verify that by getting a list of all Miss Bailey's women friends and see if Smith's description fits any of them."

"Probably got a hundred or two intimate friends," grumbled Woods, "and Smith will say they're all like the woman," for previous experiences had made Inspector Woods detest identifications of people only seen once by persons who could never notice anything really decisive in an appearance. "Or else it'll turn out to be some one she didn't see more than once in ten years."

"Well, you've had enough startling features to think about," retorted Gowing. "A little humdrum routine'll clear your brains for you."

But Woods was to be deprived of that sedative.

He was engaged next morning in interviewing Glenda Murray, who, bitterly resentful at the idea of any of their women friends being even suspected of complicity, much less of the crime itself, was not proving very helpful.

"But it's absurd, Inspector. No one we know could possibly have done anything so horrible."

"I can't go into that, Miss Murray," replied Woods patiently. "All I ask you for is a list of ladies who are on friendly terms with Miss Bailey or with yourself."

"But you know, Inspector, even if some one *had* her jewellery, it might have been all right. I mean Helen might have wanted money and asked some one to sell it for her, or she might have known some one who wanted money and let her have the things; she was awfully generous, you know, and in many ways very impulsive. It's the kind of wild thing she *might* have done. She'd not much cash of her own, you know, but she knew these things were worth a lot."

"That won't fit in with those footprints, Miss Murray. They're final, and we want to get into touch with any woman who might have made them. And I must ask you to supply the names I require." Woods spoke sternly, and Glenda was reluctantly preparing to give him the names he wished for when there came an interruption. Alan opened the door and, with a worried air, said:

"I'm obliged to interrupt you, Inspector; there's some one to see you, who says she has vital information for you." Glancing at Glenda he added, "It's Miss Eleanor Spens, a great friend of ours and a sort of cousin, in fact."

"Eleanor?" burst out Glenda. "What on earth does she know about it?"

Alan looked thoroughly uneasy, but before he could say more—

"Would you show the lady in here, please?" interrupted Woods. "Miss Murray, I'll see you again later."

He stood up and opened the door for her, giving her no option but to go, and at the same moment a woman, who had been waiting in the hall, came forward. Woods asked her to come in and sit down, and she sat down in the chair beside the desk.

Realizing that this witness promised to be one of importance, the Inspector looked at her carefully, mentally summing her up in order to decide in his own mind what weight to attach to anything she might tell him.

Eleanor Spens was a big woman, not handsome, but with a strong, clear face, full of character. Her fair hair, crisp and wavy, was barely tinged with grey, her blue eyes had a direct gaze, her complexion was of the 'open-air' type. She had at the moment an expression which Woods thought denoted rather a hard, ruthless streak in her character, but she was clearly keeping herself under severe control, which perhaps accounted for the slightly rigid determination of her mouth and jaw. She radiated efficiency and commanded the Inspector's instant recognition of the fact that here was a thoroughly competent and clear-headed witness. That she had something of importance to tell was obvious from the gravity of her manner. The Inspector prepared to listen with attention, and she began at once in a clear, almost strident, voice.

"My name is Eleanor Spens, Inspector. I am a great friend of the Murrays and I knew Helen Bailey well. I have come to you because I believe it to be my obvious duty. I believe I can give information which will lead you to her murderer—to speak accurately, her murderess." For a brief moment she looked piercingly at the Inspector, who remained in silent expectation.

She resumed more slowly, and with a deeper note in her voice:

"I had better tell you the whole situation, and to make things clear I shall have to tell you something of our family history. I am unmarried; my parents both died when I was eighteen years old. I am now forty-five, and I have devoted my life to bringing up my younger brother. He is many years younger than I am—actually, my mother died when he was born."

Glancing at her strong features and noting the sudden light which swept across them at the mention of her brother, Woods realized that here was one of those cases of a woman, lacking in sex attraction and outwardly rather unfeminine, who had the maternal instinct strongly developed, and who had turned all the deep current of her affections into her feeling for the young brother.

"We lived together," she went on, "and were extremely happy. Jack is not a strong person, either in health—or in will-power," she added rather bitterly, "and I must admit it was both a surprise and a shock to me when he suddenly married, three years ago, a girl called Mary Hookham." Her voice became expressionless as she uttered the name, but Woods realized what force she was exerting to keep her tones colourless.

"It has not been a happy marriage," she continued. "Mary Hookham was not a suitable girl for my brother to marry. She is too fond of gaiety, much too fond of bridge and dancing. She completely wore Jack out, until I was obliged to step in and show her she was ruining his nerves and his health by her late hours and perpetual restlessness."

Again she paused, and the Inspector had a momentary vision of the bitterness which lay behind the struggle of this stern woman for the health and happiness of her brother.

"I succeeded in saving Jack's health," she resumed, "but I could not, of course, change his wife's disposition. She has continued to lead her own life, and I know, Inspector, that she has gone from one extravagance to another. She is very deeply in debt, and my brother has had to notify the various shops she deals with to limit her credit. And that brings me to the point, Inspector—" she broke off, as if still further to repress her feelings, and when she resumed her tones rang coldly in his ears: "For the past three months, my brother and his wife have been on extremely bad terms. They have had frequent quarrels, mostly over money. I have myself not been on speaking terms with my sister-in-law. I was therefore surprised when, on Saturday morning, on coming in to my house at about twelve o'clock, I found a large suit-case in my front hall and a note from Mary asking me to keep the case until she should call for it. I felt angry, and saw no reason for obliging my sister-in-law. I took the suit-case out of my car and meant to take it back to her house. As I turned out of my drive, a motor-cycle dashed past right on top of me. I swerved to avoid it, hit my own gate post sideways, and tore the suit-case off the luggage grid. When I went to see what damage had been done, I found the side of the suit-case, which was only a light one, was torn open. I could see through the gap a mink fur-coat. I knew Mary had no such coat, and felt very suspicious. I thought perhaps she had bought it in defiance of her husband's check on her credit. I pulled at the edge of the coat, to make sure it was real mink and to see if it were new. When I tugged at it, something which had been rolled up underneath fell out. I pulled out a jewel-case, and in it was a pearl necklace. It had a rather remarkable diamond clasp. I knew Mary had nothing of that sort—for this was none of the imitation ones for sixpence. I felt completely astounded at this, and very uncomfortable. Indeed, I hardly knew what to do. But—" and here she spoke with great effort, and Woods realized the torments of indecision and doubt which this strong determined woman had been enduring—"I knew that I was prejudiced against my sister-in-law; I felt terribly anxious not to do her any injury or injustice. I have not wished to be the instrument of any irreparable breach between her and my brother. I felt there might be some innocent explanation of these things. My brother, I knew, was away. Mary might have been with some friend and brought away her suit-case by mistake, or they might have been involved in some accident, and she might in several ways have some explanation for her actions." A deep flush rose in her cheeks. "In any case, I shrank from being the person to expose her. I could not easily make up my mind to take advantage of my accidental discoveries. I took the suit-case back to my house, until I could decide what was best to do. It was not until this morning, when I read the description of Helen Bailey's missing things, that I realized I knew where they were. I have brought that suit-case with me, Inspector."

She stopped, having clearly said all she felt necessary. Woods wasted no time.

"Please let me have this suit-case at once," he said curtly. He followed Eleanor Spens to her car, and from the seat next the driver's lifted out a torn suit-case which had, as she described, the end torn completely out. Tied on it was a small parcel.

"I did up the jewel-case separately," said Eleanor, "as I was afraid of losing it."

They returned to the study, Woods carrying the suit-case. He undid the small parcel. It contained a most beautiful pearl necklace, one row of very large, very evenly matched pearls, with an unusual antique clasp of diamonds and topaz. Woods, who knew something of the value of these things, realized that, if genuine, it was of considerable value. The coat corresponded with the description given him by Glenda Murray—mink, with large sable collar and cuffs. It was again clearly a valuable and expensive thing, and, though it had no tab showing the shop from which it had come, it would easily be identifiable as the property of the dead woman.

For a while Woods stood looking at the suit-case and its contents. Then he came to a decision, and, turning to Eleanor:

"Miss Spens," he said. "You realize, of course, this may be a matter of the very greatest importance. I must impress on you the need for absolute silence. You must say nothing whatever about this to any one. Can I rely on you?"

"Yes, you can, Inspector," replied Eleanor firmly. "I have no wish to speak of this at all—indeed, I should have been only too thankful if I need never have come to you."

"You must not tell your brother, nor Mrs. Spens herself," continued Woods, who had decided on a plan of action. "Mrs. Spens may not come back to you for the case for a day or two. If she should call for it, I think the only thing is for you to be away. Can you arrange to go away for one of two days, at once? I am sorry to inconvenience you, but I need a little time, and this seems the best way to gain it. If you can go away until next Monday, and leave word with your maids that you have locked the case away somewhere, Mrs. Spens will probably leave the matter over till you return."

"Yes," said Eleanor. "I can manage that quite well. I usually keep my deed boxes and so on locked into a small spare room, of which I keep the key. It would be perfectly natural for me to put this case in there, or rather," she corrected herself, "let my maids have the impression it is in there. And if I am expected home very shortly, Mary would, of course, have to wait till I was back."

"Very well," acquiesced Woods. "I see I can trust you, Miss Spens, but I must repeat once more that this matter is vitally important, and I can assure you a great deal will turn on your absolute discretion and silence for the next day or two."

Looking at her grave face, he saw that she understood all the implications of the affair, and felt no more need be said. He wrote out a brief account of the circumstances in which Eleanor had come into possession of the suit-case, which she signed, and she then departed.

Chapter VIII

THE BLUE BOX

"The evidence that do accuse me"

Richard III.

L eft to himself, Woods sent for Riley. Briefly he told him of the finding of the coat and necklace.

"Now, Riley," he said, "I don't want to act openly on this just yet. I might go and interrogate Mrs. Spens and ask her to account for having these things in her possession. But it would be easy enough for her to tell some tale. Her sister-in-law saw that for herself. She might say that Miss Bailey asked her to keep them—or to sell them for her—and we couldn't prove anything to the contrary. It would show her we were on her track, and that I must try to avoid for the present."

"Why?" asked Riley. "What great harm would be done if she did know we'd traced these things to her? If she's mixed up in this, a little fright and apprehension might make her give herself away—whereas, if she's innocent, no harm's done."

"No," replied Woods. "See here. This is a big affair, and we can't make any mistakes. We've got to have clear, definite proof before we charge any one with this murder. Now, of course, to be found in possession of the murdered woman's things, when it's known from those footprints that a woman was at least present at the scene of the crime, is of course a very strong presumption of guilt. But it's not proof. We need more evidence—and, as I see it, if we're not very careful we'll alarm Mrs. Spens—and her husband—and give them the chance to destroy the proofs we are seeking."

"You're thinking of her own clothes," said Riley acutely, "on the assumption that they're bloodstained?"

"Yes, I am. We know from the medical evidence that whoever stooped over that poor woman as she lay on the floor, slashing at her, must have been pretty well covered with blood. We can assume also that the murderer's shoes would be stained too—from the pool of blood there was on the floor—the traces showed that, even though they'd been partially washed out."

"Now, assuming the guilty person was a woman, a thin frock stains very easily—her underclothes, as well as her dress, were probably marked. If it were a man, well, his thicker clothes would be even more difficult to get rid of afterwards. Man or woman, the problem of getting rid of certainly bloodstained clothes, and possibly bloodstained shoes, isn't an easy one. You can't burn a dress without leaving a good deal of ash, and perhaps traces of fasteners or buttons or what not. Now it's possible that if Mrs. Spens or her husband are concerned in this—we mustn't, of course, assume just yet she's guilty—but if she is, he may be helping her to try and escape the consequences—they've either not got rid of the stained clothes, or, in doing so, they may have left traces of what they've done."

Woods paused, and Riley, who had listened intently, nodded to show his agreement so far.

"Then," proceeded Woods, "the first thing we must do is to search the Spens' house and garden. We don't want them to know what we're up to, if it can possibly be prevented. I want you to go along there now and just see how the land lies. I've gathered from the sister, Miss Spens, things aren't any too happy there. With luck you may find they're away or out a good deal. Take one of our women along with you, and get her to go through the wardrobes and make a list of all the dresses you find there. We may be able, if all else fails, to track down her dresses and find something's missing and can't be accounted for. Then, go over the dust-bins, of course, and have a good, thorough search for anything likely to help us. I doubt if you'll find anything in the nature of the stained clothes themselves, but you may find something that'll lead us to them. And don't lose time, for I don't want her or him to suspect we've anything against them—it would only egg them on to get rid of anything incriminating they may have kept."

With these instructions Riley set out. It did not take him long to reach the small but attractive house where the Spens lived. Deciding to pose as one of the innumerable men who frequent suburban houses selling silk stockings, or notepaper, brushes, and so on, he advanced up the neat, well-kept path to the front door. He knocked and rang in vain, and at this moment the milkman passed the gate, and seeing him, shouted out, "No use knocking there—family away." Retracing his steps down the path, Riley inquired of the man "if everyone were away in this road; it was the third house he'd been to and all shut up." The milkman only stared at him suspiciously and, feeling that if he loitered he would probably find himself reported to the police as a bad character, Riley walked briskly away in the direction of the next road, which led to the Tube. He actually went back to the police station and, later in the evening, having collected two men and the woman detective as helpers, they went back to the Spens' house in a band. This time they found the road free from all tradesmen and passers-by, and, as it was a quiet place, with no through traffic, there was little chance of their being observed. The Spens' house was detached from its neighbours, and had been built on a site carved out of one of the ancient woods still remaining on the Highstead hills. A thick belt of old oaks sheltered the Spens from their neighbours on either side, while at the back the garden sloped down into what was quite a forest. The fact that in this way none of the rooms could be overlooked had recommended it to Jack and Mary, and it now proved an equal satisfaction to Sergeant Riley and his helpers. They rapidly broke through the very simple and flimsy bolts and bars of the French window leading from the drawing-room on to the lawn. Once inside, they dared not turn up the lights, but their own lamps and flashes were sufficient, since the search they were to conduct did not require any very minute inspection. While Riley himself went up to the top floor where the bedrooms lay, accompanied by Miss Merson and one of the detectives, two others set to work to inspect the kitchen premises and the ash-bin, and to search the small, beautifully neat garden for any traces of a bonfire, or of recent digging.

At the end of a couple of hours of careful and painstaking investigation, nothing had been found. "Nothing whatever," said Detective Woodrow briefly, in reporting to Riley. "Everything's in apple-pie order. The dustbin was full—that was one piece of luck—the scavengers must be due to-morrow, but there's nothing whatever suspicious in it. We've sieved all the dust from the fire-places, no great amount. The house is all run by electricity—only one open fire in the place, and that's not been used this week. No sign of anything having been burnt in the garden, and not a sign of digging. Nothing unusual in any of the cupboards or drawers. In fact, not a sign in our part of anything out of the ordinary whatever."

"We've had no better luck either," replied Riley. "All's tidy upstairs—can't of course say what's there and what's gone. I've got a list of all the suits, boots and shoes and so on in Mr. Spens' room, and we've also got a complete one of Mrs. Spens' dresses and coats—a nice long one it is too—an extravagant young woman she must be! I've given special attention to the boxroom, but there's nothing *in* the house, that I'll swear. If there was ever anything to be concealed, it's been taken out."

At this moment Miss Merson came into the room.

"I had an idea, Sergeant," she said, "and it's borne fruit." She held out to Riley a small crumpled piece of paper. "I've been going through her purse-bags, thinking it possible, if she'd anything to get rid of, she'd fall for the old trick of the left luggage, and that she might have left the check-ticket in one of her bags. Sure enough. I've found this—a check-ticket for a bag left in the parcels office at Charing Cross."

"What date?" said Riley eagerly, taking the little scrap of paper from her.

"July 8th, that's Saturday," replied Miss Merson. They all looked at each other.

"Well, well," said Riley cynically. "They never seem to learn."

Stowing away the precious scrap, they made sure no traces of their visit were left to warn the owners of the house, and, after closing and relocking the French window, they silently made their way out of the garden and along the quiet road. Riley went back to the police station to make his report, for, despite the lateness of the hour, he realized this clue was of sufficient importance to be given immediate attention.

But when, the next day, accompanied by Woods himself, he visited the Parcels Office at Charing Cross station, it was only to meet with a check. The clerk, on being shown Woods' official card and the counterfoil, readily produced the article which had been deposited on the Saturday morning. It was a small old shabby leather bag, of the kind people used to dispatch with small boys and girls on their way to boarding school, containing the said children's gear for the first night before heavy boxes were unpacked. They took the bag off to the office attached to the parcels hall, and, with the help of Woods' pocket tools, it was soon unlocked. It was empty; nothing whatever lay within, not even a scrap of paper. The two men looked at each other with a feeling of bitter disappointment. Woods had been more deeply impressed than he had admitted, even to himself, by the discovery of the coat and necklace. He had hoped, though not very confidently, that the traces of further complicity might be found in the Spens' house. The discovery of the check-ticket, with the very date to be expected, had made him sure that he was on the verge of a great discovery. Now his hopes were dashed.

Bending closely over the bag, he was able to see a few faint dark smears in one corner on the blue and white striped cotton lining. Flashing on his torch, the bright beam showed up the marks distinctly.

"We'll have these analysed," he remarked to Riley. Then, turning to the clerk, "Do you remember anything about the person depositing this bag?"

"Why, yes," answered the young man. "I do. She—it was a lady—brought it in first early on Saturday."

"What was the time?" queried Woods.

"Just before 9.30, I should say," answered the clerk. "I know it was before 9.45, as we've a lot of trains in about then, and I've a regular rush hour till about 10.15. She came in when I wasn't very busy, for I noticed her appearance as not fitting in with this bag."

"What do you mean by that?" said Woods sharply.

"Well, you can see for yourself this is a shabby, old-fashioned sort of thing," returned the clerk, "and she wasn't anything of the sort. Very smart and up-to-date she was, made up and all that—very well dressed. I couldn't think how she'd like to be seen carrying this queer old bag—it spoilt her whole appearance."

"Would you know her again?"

The clerk hesitated. "Don't altogether know that I would. I might. She was young, and I think dark, but I couldn't really describe her much. It was chiefly her smart clothes I noticed, and I'd not have thought them very unusual if it hadn't been for any one like that carrying a bag like this."

Woods' heart sank. Once more he realized how difficult a task is identification, especially at a London terminus, where scores of well-dressed young women, all turned out in what, to the male eye, appears much the same style, flow backwards and forwards in the stream of passengers. Then his mind reverted to a phrase the clerk had used. "You said the lady brought it in first, early on Saturday?"

"Yes," answered the official. "I mean, she came first of all with this bag early on Saturday morning. But I ought to have explained that's not the original ticket. She came back again, and that's the ticket she had for this bag the second time."

"Just explain that," said Woods patiently, realizing that he must neither hustle or muddle this witness if he were to get accurate information.

"Well, it was like this. She came back again that afternoon, at about two o'clock. She'd got one of those light, coloured, round hat boxes with her; the kind ladies carry over their arms nowadays. It was a bright blue, I remember. She came and fetched this bag and went off to the ladies' cloak-room over in the corner there. I saw her go down the stairs that lead to it. About a quarter of an hour later she came back, said she didn't think she could manage to carry the two things after all, so she'd put this in again. So I issued her another check, and that's actually the one you've got there."

Woods listened to this explanation with increasing gloom. He saw clearly what had been done. Mary Spens had hurried out of her house at that early hour, taking with her, he now felt sure, something she wished to conceal, and surely that something must have been the stained frock he visualized when he mentally reconstructed the scene of the murder. A thin evening frock, and other things as well, would easily have been compressed into that bag. He knew she must have been hurrying to the jewellers to get rid of some at least of the incriminating articles and probably to secure the money she so badly needed. She would not wish to take with her anything marked with her initials, such as her dressing-case or a suit-case. If she were intending to leave her dangerous parcel at a parcels office, and if, as he realized was probable, those garments were still wet with blood, she would not dare to risk a mere cardboard box. This little old bag, a relic of earlier days, would have seemed to her at first ideal. She would snatch it up, from wherever it had been put away, and hurry as fast as she could to get these things away from her house. Then, perhaps, she had realized before she reached the railway terminus, that this odd little bag was calling attention to her. Others besides the clerk had probably stared at the incongruity of such a girl carrying such a bag. She had perhaps reflected on the matter while she did her other business. She would decide that she dared not leave the bag with the dangerous contents, lest the parcels clerk had noticed her appearance and could describe it. If he were correct in his deductions, she had gone from the station to the jewellers, not five minutes away by taxi. Then she must have gone back to her home to collect the large suit-case containing the fur coat and necklace. He wondered at first why that suit-case too had not been deposited in the lost luggage, and then realized it had embossed upon it her initials and was covered with the pictorial labels of foreign hotels. She had been clever enough to perceive such a case would have been easily identified and traced, when not claimed, and would have led direct back to her. He knew she had left that suit-case, known and identifiable as hers, at Eleanor Spens' house before noon. Then she must have planned out this further step with regard to the little bag, had returned to the parcels office, claimed it, gone to the ladies' room, and there transferred its contents, whatever they were, to the blue hat-box. She had then got rid of the little bag by depositing it once more, and had thereby saved herself for the time being. Whether the clerk could describe her or not would be immaterial, for the bag contained nothing dangerous now. What, then, could she have done with its contents? Quite clearly Woods realized he had come to a dead end. Instructing the clerk to keep the bag on one side, and, if any one should claim it, to notify a plain-clothes man, who would be stationed at hand, he went back to his office to try and think out his next move.

Chapter IX

THE ARREST

"Come, let's away to prison"

King Lear.

Woods possessed imagination, and he now set to work to use this quality in trying to uncover the next piece of the trail, which, he hoped, would lead him to the definite evidence he was seeking.

Retracing the progress already made, he mentally decided he need now have no real doubt that Mary was guilty of at least complicity in the crime. She answered too well to the known facts respecting the woman who had been at "The Towers" on Friday night. She was an intimate friend of the Murrays. She was on intimate terms with Helen Bailey. She had left her home in the morning after a violent quarrel with her husband, and had gone to the Murrays with the avowed intention of obtaining money or help from Helen. All that was definitely known and could be proved.

The next link was the finding of Helen's coat and necklace in her possession, or, to be accurate, the tracing those articles to her. This, through the instrumentality of her sister-in-law, Eleanor, had been achieved. At this point Woods realized how much he owed to the spirit which had prompted Eleanor to come to him with her tale. Had it not been for her, he would never have had his attention drawn to Mary, or, rather, he must have had her name supplied to him as one of Helen's intimates, but nothing would have connected her with the crime. Thanks to Eleanor, he now had a very strong link forged between her and the murder. Whether Eleanor had really been actuated by a sense of duty and of citizenship, Woods in his heart rather doubted. He knew too much of human nature, and was fairly confident that, had Eleanor loved her brother's wife, she would possibly have shielded her, and most probably held her tongue. But she had made no pretence; she had admitted that she disliked Mary, and for that honesty Woods gave her credit. Anyhow, thanks to her, Mary did now definitely come under suspicion. Woods felt hopeful that the jewellers' assistants would be able to identify her; he hoped the railway clerk might do the same. Their identifications were, however, only needed as a formality. Woods himself had no doubts that it was indeed Mary who had sold the jewellery, and Mary who had deposited the now empty bag. He was equally sure that his efforts must now be concentrated on solving the problem of what she had done with the blue hat-box.

At this stage, his imagination came to his aid. He put himself in Mary's place, pretending he was trying, as she would do, to dispose of that little old bag. She must have felt the risk too great to leave it with its contents. If traced to her, she must be able to prove it harmless. Therefore, the contents must be transferred to something not so easily identifiable with her. Something brand new would be best, and at once Woods realized that not a stone's throw from the station, in the Strand, were plenty of shops selling suit-cases, hat-boxes, and luggage of all descriptions. He picked up his telephone and gave directions that every shop in the neighbourhood of Charing Cross should be visited, to ascertain if any had sold a bright blue, light, American cloth hat-box on Saturday morning. At the same time he sent for the man whom he had put on to find out everything that could be discovered as to Mary's movements and her present whereabouts.

From the report made by the detective to whom this job had been allotted, Woods soon learnt that Mary had been at home alone on Friday and on the Saturday. Her husband had gone to Norfolk on Friday afternoon. She had stayed behind, but he had returned on the Sunday evening. They had both gone down to the South Coast on Monday evening, and were expected back that very day.

"I've got a man watching the house, sir, and he'll report when they return, and I've arranged to put on an extra man and have them both shadowed."

Woods nodded, and, dismissing his subordinate, prepared to wait for further news. But, as he picked up his pen to tabulate the results of his efforts, a fresh idea struck him. He knew Mary had not deposited the blue hat box at Charing Cross, but perhaps she had simply taken it elsewhere, or, as an alternative, had dispatched it as a parcel to be forwarded by rail somewhere else. Here Woods saw another possible line of research, and at once gave directions for inquiry to be made at the various termini along these lines.

Two hours later he realized his luck was in. Reports came promptly to hand. A young lady, answering to Mary's description, had bought the blue hat-box at the shop almost opposite the station. She had asked if it were waterproof, a query that to Woods seemed slightly ominous, for it seemed to bear out the theory that whatever was destined to go in that hat-box was wet or damp. Next, the luggage-in-advance department at Charing Cross itself reported that a lady had come in at 2.30, had shown a ticket for Bardsley, a country station about twenty miles down the line, and had dispatched a blue hat-box to that station, to be left there till called for. She had given the name as "Mrs. Stanton."

Sure that he was on the right track, Woods himself decided to set off for Bardsley, for he felt this was the most important part of the investigation. Everything turned on tracing the missing clothes; there was nothing at the London end of equal importance.

Bardsley proved a small country village, with a small station. Big houses and villas lay farther out, scattered among the low hills and along the road, and from them came enough "daily breaders" to make the station busy in the morning and evening hours. In the middle of the day, however, there was little traffic, and Woods found the stationmaster unoccupied. Going through with him to the little office where parcels were both received and dispatched, Woods soon obtained the information he wanted. The hat-box had duly arrived on the previous Saturday. It had remained in the office until Monday; indeed, it could not have been removed on the Sunday, for the parcels office was closed. On Monday, at about 11 o'clock, a young lady, slight and dark, quietly dressed, had come and inquired for it. She had paid the dues on it and gone away, carrying it over her arm. The porter had taken note of the incident, for the hat-box was of the light, flimsy, crushable variety, and he had been surprised at it being sent by "luggage in advance". He had jokingly told the young lady she should have sent it by passenger train, and she had seemed confused, and hesitated, and eventually said she "had not thought of that." The porter had also noticed the same young lady waiting for the up-train an hour later. She was no longer carrying the case, and the porter had vaguely surmised she had left it with some friend in the locality. He had noticed it was quite new, but it had not been empty. It had been secured with string tied carefully and tightly, so that it would take time to undo.

Woods at once set out in the direction which he ascertained the girl had taken when she left the station. She had chosen the road leading away from the village and going in the direction of the Downs. He realized that she must have been pressed for time. He did not believe for an instant she had left the case with any friend.

This was not a locked suit-case, but a very flimsy affair, with no fastenings but a couple of clips and the string, which would prevent an idle porter from peeping in, but would give no real security. He was sure she had hidden it somewhere near at hand. Roughly calculating how far she would have gone in order to return and catch the next up train within the hour, he walked along looking anxiously for any likely place. He decided she would not utilize the very first possible cover, such as the thick hedge or a clump of bushes, but would try to find something really secure. For a while the road mounted steeply, bordered with occasional villas and garden walls. Then he came to the top of the hill, and left the villas behind him. Here it was open country. On his left a little side-road ran off, leading in the near distance to a small wood. He felt that to be a likely spot, and turned in that direction, passing a small cottage, where two little boys were swinging on a gate and calling to their dog. Walking briskly to the wood, the Inspector found it a thick copse, with a good number of large trees and very tangled undergrowth, intersected by a regular little maze of paths. As he hesitated which to follow, he heard a sharp bark behind him, and saw that the small urchins and their mongrel had followed him at a discreet distance. An idea occurred to him. Beckoning to the elder boy, and holding up a sixpence he said:

"Would you like to help me to look for something?"

The boy promptly nodded and came up at once.

"I want you and your brother to help me to look for something which may be in this wood," began the inspector, "a bright blue box—a sort of hat-box, I mean."

"Do you mean the one the lady hid on Monday?" replied the boy.

Woods felt his heart positively jump.

"That may be it," he said quietly. "What did the lady do with hers, and what was it like?"

"Well," said the boy, who was perfectly ready to talk, "she came up here on Monday morning before dinner-time. Dick and I were up here in the wood playing about and noticed her walking along. She'd one of them new cases like you see ladies have, a bright blue one, hung over her arm. We went scouting along through the trees, just for fun, following her, and she never saw us at all. When she got a good way in she turned off the path and went along by the big fallen tree, and we watched and, after a bit, we saw her kneeling down covering up her case. She covered it all up with dirt and sticks and leaves and things and then came away."

"Well," said the Inspector, sure that there was more to come, "what did you do? I'll bet you didn't come away and leave that case without having a look inside it?"

The boy grinned. "No, sir, we went and had a lock, because we thought she might have been burying some bits of a body, like people do in a murder case, but there wasn't anything like that, only some spoilt clothes, that wouldn't be any good to any one."

"And what did you do with them?" asked Woods, filled with horror lest the boys should by any chance have destroyed them.

"Oh well, they were all marked and spoilt and wet, so we just shoved them all under the tree root again, and I took the case home for Mum—it was quite new, and I saw the lady didn't want it."

"Can you show me where you left the clothes?"

"Why, yes, it's only a short bit from here," and, running ahead along a little twisting path, followed by the Inspector, the boy soon pointed out a large fallen tree, which lay a short way off the track. Pushing aside the bracken and greenery which had sprung up round the cavity formed by its roots, Woods plunged his hand into a hole scooped out obviously by the hand of man, and from it withdrew a crumpled bundle of clothing.

"Is this what you found in the case?" he asked the boy.

"Yes, sir."

"Exactly as you put it back here?"

"Yes, sir."

"How old are you?"

"Ten and two months, sir."

"Ever been to a police court?"

The boy, who had looked increasingly uneasy, turned pale and hesitated.

"Don't be afraid. You've done nothing wrong at all. I only want to know if you've ever heard any one give evidence in a court of law."

The boy looked relieved and his face lightened.

"Oh yes, sir, and if you want me to give evidence"—with mounting enthusiasm—"I'll come along and say all about it, sir. I know what an oath is right enough."

Woods was satisfied he could really produce the boy if necessary to prove the facts as to the bundle having come out of the blue case, and the case itself he could of course recover from the boy's mother. So, with a feeling of having carried out successfully a tiresome piece of work, he unrolled the bundle and spread its contents out in the dappled sunshine on the big root of the tree.

He shook out first of all a thin black sleeveless frock. It was made of some flimsy material, and the whole front of the skirt, from the waist downwards, was stained and stiff with what his practised eye knew to be dried blood. Besides the frock there was a thin, black silk slip, also deeply stained down the front, and a pair of very fine silk stockings. The stockings appeared to have been partially washed. They were stained below the knee, but the feet and the parts just above the ankles were not so much marked, and the general appearance of discoloration gave the impression that they had been roughly soaked in water. Finally, there was a pair of black satin slippers, very high heeled, with tiny, expensive looking diamond clasps to their straps. They had a few dark brown splashes and smears upon them, but these were only faintly visible. The shoes again, however, looked as if they had been soaked in water, for they were cockled and misshapen and had shrunk in places.

The two boys had watched awe-struck while the Inspector made his examination. Obviously bursting with the desire to speak, they were held in restraint by the grim, stern look which had come over the man's face. When he had finished, and had made sure that nothing further remained in the hole beneath the tree, the Inspector rolled up the clothes once more, put them inside his own attaché case, which he locked, and then, turning to the two boys, he said:

"Well, I'm glad you didn't take that bundle home to your mother to be used for rags. Come along now and take me to her, I'll need to ask her for that hat-box."

Something in his tones kept the boys from venturing on any remarks, and it was a silent trio which retraced its steps to the cottage by the wayside.

Three hours later Woods stood before the door of the small villa belonging to Jack Spens. In answer to his ring, a cheerful, stout charlady opened the door, and, on hearing he wished to see Mrs. Spens, ushered him into the little drawing-room. Two people were sitting there—a young man of about twenty-five and a girl rather younger. As he looked at the young man, Eleanor's expression "not strong either physically or in will-power" sprang to Woods' mind. Jack Spens was extremely good-looking in a very delicate effeminate way. His golden hair had the wave beloved of film-stars, his eyes were large and blue. He looked gentle, refined, but obviously had no stamina, and was equally clearly in a state of nervous tension. Nor did his wife, whom Woods had, of course, never seen hitherto, look either well or happy. He noticed that she was slim and slightly made, with small wrists and hands and feet. Again, involuntarily, a phrase flashed through Woods' mind, the medical report, "the blows were struck either by an old man or by a woman," and yet, glancing at her face, he felt a pang of incredulity. Surely this girl could not by any possibility have committed this crime?

Mary Spens was looking at that moment especially beautiful in a soft dim style. Her dark hair was very smooth and shining; her face was small and pointed and was lit by a pair of grey eyes that seemed at the moment to be almost too big for her face. For even her make-up could not hide the dark smudgy shadows beneath her eyes, and nothing could conceal the look of terror that came into them as the Inspector announced his name.

"I am sorry to cause you trouble, madam," he said, turning to Mary, "but I come from Scotland Yard and must ask you some questions in connexion with the murder of Miss Helen Bailey."

Mary clearly summoned all her self-control and her face seemed to stiffen with resolve as she replied, "Of course, Inspector, I knew Helen Bailey well, but I am afraid I cannot tell you anything as to her death."

"I must, madam, please ask you to give me certain information. To begin with, where were you on Friday, July 6th, at 4 P.M.?"

"I was here, at home."

"Can you prove that?" A brief pause followed. Then:

"No. I was alone. My husband was away, and there was no one else in the house."

"Where were you during that evening, especially from 7 P.M. onwards?"

"I dined at a restaurant and went to the theatre with a friend, who can prove I was with her from 7.30 to just after 11."

"After that, where were you?"

"I came home here."

"Did you have a taxi?"

"No, I was driving my own car."

Turning to Jack Spens, who had sat in silent horror during this dialogue, Woods asked him:

"Can you confirm any of this, Mr. Spens?"

"No, I was away for the week-end," stammered the young man.

"Can your maids corroborate it?"

"No," said Mary defiantly. "We have no maid sleeping in. I was alone in the house."

A longer pause followed, and then the Inspector turned to the case, which he had deposited on the floor beside his chair. He opened it, and drew out the stained frock, stockings and shoes. As her eyes fell on them, Mary's face grew absolutely ghastly.

"Are these your property, madam?" said the inspector slowly.

Mary could not answer. Turning sternly to her husband, the Inspector put the question to him.

"Mr. Spens, do you recognize these things?"

Jack looked wildly at his wife, then back at the Inspector. With a shaking hand he picked up one of the satin slippers. Some brief struggle appeared on his face, and then, as if overborne by the Inspector's grim determination to get at the truth, he hoarsely answered:

"Yes, I identify them as belonging to my wife."

Two hours later Mary Spens entered the doors of Holloway Gaol, charged with the murder of Helen Bailey.

Chapter X

THE TRIAL

"Devoid of pity, and being so shall have like want of pity"

Titus Andronicus.

The trial of Mary Spens for the wilful murder of Helen Bailey had already lasted two days, and Inspector Woods felt unutterably weary as he left the court.

"Well, to-morrow will see it done with," he thought as he pushed his way through the swarming, jostling crowd. Disgust welled up as he listened to the comments of the people round him. The case had attracted immense interest, as indeed he had foreseen the very moment he opened the suit-case brought by Eleanor Spens. The wealth and position of the Murrays had, in the first place, focused attention on the murder. Then natural horror had risen over the circumstances of the crime, and the horrible details as to the injuries inflicted; excitement had been roused by the arrest of a young and attractive woman; and finally the personality of the accused had deepened the public interest in the case.

As he sat at home that evening, glancing through the notes he had made in court, Woods sank into a reverie, thinking of the figure of Mary in the dock and, despite his strong common sense and his experience that often appearances gave a wrong clue to character, he wondered how Mary Spens could ever have brought herself to the murder of her friend. Before his eyes he seemed to see once more her small slight figure, as she had sat wearily hour after hour in that dock, very pale, with a look of incredulous misery stamped on her face, drooping, apparently broken with the horror of her situation. To the spectators the futility of her defence seemed to be almost pathetic—the case she had had to meet almost appalling in its strength.

The case presented by the prosecution had been straightforward enough. The Murray family had for years been on the most intimate terms with both Jack and Eleanor Spens, and as Mary Hookham Mary had as a child shared Glenda's lessons and been taught by Helen Bailey. Glenda had been one of Mary's bridesmaids. Helen had always been specially fond of Mary and, when Mary's marriage began to lead to trouble, Helen had taken Mary's side in the quarrels with Jack and Eleanor, declaring that Mary's position was intolerable with Eleanor's jealous interference continually breaking in upon her married life.

It was proved that Mary was heavily in debt. Her husband, supported by his sister, had refused to pay her debts, and told her she must raise the money herself to pay her creditors. Mary had realized most of her small capital, for she did not apparently wish to make public her position by allowing her husband to be sued for her debts. She had tried speculating, but had only met with ill success and increased her difficulties. The situation had become intolerable, the quarrels more and more embittered.

Counsel for the prosecution had drawn a picture of Mary rushing from her home early on the Friday morning after her violent quarrel at breakfast with her husband and going over to "The Towers." Her known movements were then traced, and the story was told of the next definite thing she admitted having done, namely her appearance at Eleanor Spens' house with the suit-case. The opening of that suit-case was described and its fatal contents. It was proved by Glenda Murray's unwilling evidence that the coat and necklace had belonged to Helen Bailey. The black evening frock and slip were alleged to be Mary's. The length of the frock, when worn by a woman of Mary's height, was measured against the door of Helen's bedroom, and it was shown that the blood-soaked hem, if brushed against the door by a person wearing that frock passing out of the room would make a smear at the exact place where the stain was found on the painted lower panel. The stockings and shoes were also of the size worn by Mary.

Evidence would be produced to show that Helen, in opposition to the Victorian air of her sitting-room, had used a mahogany cupboard as a miniature cocktail bar. Glenda and Alan were obliged to admit that they frequently went to her room for cocktails, before lunch or dinner. On the fatal Friday they had had cocktails before their start for the country. Helen had opened a fresh bottle of Vermouth, which was practically empty when the detectives searched the room on Monday night. A bottle of brandy was also found empty. Mary had often joined them in Helen's room, and knew of the cocktail cupboard and of the place where Helen kept the key. She had not been at "The Towers" for lunch or dinner during that week, but on the bottle of brandy and on one of the glasses her finger-prints were found.

The prosecution from this drew a picture of Mary, returning to the house during the afternoon when she knew Helen was alone, of her drinking cocktail after cocktail, and gradually working herself up into a wild state of excitement over her difficulties and her need for money, of her quarrelling with her friend, and in a frenzy doing a deed which, in her sober senses, she could never have accomplished. The weapon, it was alleged, was a small steel axe, part of a set of fireside tools, hanging on a stand on the hearth, making the figure and the equipment of a "man in armour." The axe was about two feet long, the blade of the head being fairly sharp, the base of it weighted to form a poker. It had been wiped clean of finger-prints and everything else, but a few minute stains at the place where the blade of the axe joined the shaft were declared by experts to be human blood. It was also proved that the nature of the injuries was consistent with the use of this weapon.

The tracing of the bag and hat-box, and the finding of the bloodstained clothes was described, and the sale of the other items of jewellery. The prosecution thus claimed to show motive and opportunity to prove the identity of Mary with the murderer.

Mary's answer was a complete and total denial of the charge.

I I

Then had come the procession of witnesses. First James Murray had entered the box. His tall, erect figure, his thin brown eagle-face beneath its thatch of grey hair, and, above all, the strange bright gleam of his extraordinary blue eyes, made his entry most impressive. He gave his evidence clearly but dryly, evidently resenting the horrible publicity in which he and his family were involved. His statements were colourless but to the point. He was the last person who had seen Helen Bailey alive. He described how he had gone out, leaving her alone in the house, with the door put on the chain behind him. He had previously gone into her sitting-room to tell her he would probably not be back to tea, and he was sure no fire had then been lit. He gave an account of his return, of the finding of the note in the hall, of his efforts to open the doors of Helen's bed and sitting rooms. He described his solitary week-end in the house, and the return of his son and grandson on the Monday. He described their discovery that the spare-room key would open the sitting-room door, their joint entry into the rooms on the first floor, and their finding of the body. Though none of this evidence was of first-rate importance, yet a good deal of interest was taken in this witness, for it was vaguely known that at one time he had been regarded with some suspicion by the police. His age, and his very striking appearance, also helped to focus attention upon him, and he won more favour than his son John, who seemed an uninteresting person, lacking in force and individuality besides the old man. John could merely corroborate that part of his father's evidence relating to their entry into Helen's room and the finding of her body.

Then had come the evidence of the doctors. As the details they gave became clear, a wave of horror and of animus against the prisoner in the dock could have been felt beating through the packed court. The numerous and terrible injuries inflicted—the fact that two attacks had been made, that the murdered woman had revived after the first onslaught, had been again attacked as she lay on the ground, had in vain tried to ward off the rain of blows with her hands, and had eventually been slashed and battered to death—all this was heard in appalled silence. Then came the account by Dr. James of the attempts to identify the now famous bloody footprints. He described how those prints appeared clear and distinct upon the Japanese matting. "They were the prints of a bare foot, showing the heel, a high instep, and the toes, all perfectly distinct and fully apparent." The measurements from toe to heel had been most carefully taken. "They did not in any way correspond with those of Helen Bailey, whose feet were longer, broader, and bigger in every respect." Nor had they the slightest resemblance with those of Mr. James Murray. The footprints left in the room were made by a person with a high instep; Mr. Murray had, it turned out, flat feet, and his foot in general was very much longer and larger, and indeed gave totally different measurements.

Dr. James then described how he had tried to obtain from Mary Spens' foot accurate prints which could be compared with those in the room. He had first tried various chemical substances, but none of them proved suitable. Realizing that only from blood could he obtain satisfactory prints, he had obtained some bullock's blood, put it in a shallow bowl, and then asked Mary Spens to dip her bare foot in the bowl and walk across some matting. Mary had apparently been perfectly willing to carry out the tests. The result of the experiment was the production of prints which exactly resembled those on the mat. The size, shape, the gap left by the high arch, all were exact in every particular.

A distinct gasp had gone through the court at this passage in the evidence. Many wondered how any woman could have borne to dip her bare foot in that horrible bowl, even if innocent, while to a guilty person it must have seemed as if once more she were walking in the blood of the dead woman.

This similarity of the prints seemed perfectly conclusive. A hush fell as the doctor concluded his evidence. The Superintendent remarked to Inspector Woods:

"That clinched it—there was no getting away from *that*."

III

Yet Mary's counsel had tried desperately to get away from it. The defence was a total denial that she had ever laid a finger on her friend, or indeed that she had been back again to see her at "The Towers" on that Friday. The story told on her behalf was this:—She had found her life intolerable, between her husband, dominated by his elder sister, and that sister. Constant interference, and the perpetual friction, had driven her to despair. She had at last decided to leave her husband, and had confided in Helen. Helen had warmly supported her, and had promised to help her. She had indeed told Mary that she would let her have £500. On Mary asking how she could spare such a sum, Helen had replied she had not the actual money, but she had got some valuable jewellery, which she would let Mary have, and which could either be sold or, perhaps, pawned. Mary intended to set up a shop, for she was very clever at clothes, and she hoped to be able to pay back the loan fairly soon.

She had talked it all over finally with Helen on the Friday morning, and Helen had then told her that she had decided to break with her ancient admirer, Mr. Scott and had no wish to keep any of his presents. He had refused to take them back and said she had no reason to return them as there had never been any engagement to marry and the gifts were quite unconditional. She had told Mary to sell or pawn the jewellery and to try to sell the fur coat. Mary had accordingly taken the things away on Friday morning, unobserved by the Murrays. Hearing early on the Monday of the murder, she had been panic-stricken, and her first impulse had been to take back the things to "The Towers." She had then reflected that with Helen dead, she had no hope of help from her, and, being completely desperate, had resolved to sell the jewellery and try to secure funds, believing Helen herself would have wished this. Realizing the coat would be, as she thought, more easily traced, she had wished to get it out of her house lest her husband should see it on his return, and, time being precious, and having no one else near enough, had risked her sister-in-law's enmity, relying on her belief that Eleanor would never open a locked case.

As to the footprints, her counsel declared, and brought other medical experts to support his contention, that, though the footprints obtained from Mary's foot did very closely resemble those found in the room, yet, as no study of naked footprints had hitherto been made, it was impossible to consider it proved beyond doubt that the prints might not have been made by another woman of similar build.

Up to this point, those experienced in the ways of criminal trials felt that, however strong the presumption of guilt, the Crown had not so far fully proved its case.

When, however, the question of the bloodstained clothes found in the suit-case came up, excitement rose. In the first place, the stains were peculiar, in that the silk under-slip, and the frock, while widely stained from the waist downwards, had no stains above the waist. Even the bodice of the frock was practically unspotted, and, as Counsel for the defence emphasized, any person standing over a prostrate body and slashing at the big artery in the neck, which had been cut, must have been covered with the blood spouting from the wounds. Nor was it possible to assert that that the prisoner had worn a coat, for all her coats existed and had been identified, and all were quite free from stains. Furthermore her ownership of the frock and slip were denied, and it proved impossible to identify them as hers. Jack Spens, who had admitted to the Inspector that he identified them, was now in a state of complete collapse, installed with a nurse in Eleanor's house, and he took advantage of the proviso that a husband cannot be forced to give evidence against his wife to refuse to appear in court. Eleanor Spens had seen too little of her sister-in-law to be able to swear to her clothes, nor, it transpired, could any one else. And, as Woods had foreseen, it was not possible to obtain identification of Mary with the girl who had bought the blue hat-box and deposited the shabby bag at the parcels office at Charing Cross.

The assistant at the luggage shop had completely failed to pick her out at an identification parade, and the parcels clerk proved equally unsuccessful.

It was, therefore, essential to prove beyond doubt that the actual garments found in the hat-box belonged to Mary, and here her counsel was able to put up a good fight on her behalf. The black frock was produced in court. It was, to the male eye certainly, quite inconspicuous, being very plainly made, though beautifully cut, and with no special ornament or distinctive features. Counsel for the defence took the line that it was not Mary's dress at all. He went on to prove that Mary had a great number of dresses, and no one could be produced to say positively that the one in question was amongst them. Mary had in her wardrobe eighteen evening and dinner frocks. The judge, in accordance with the apparently fixed resolve of justice to maintain that it is never abreast of modern life, appeared completely stunned by this statement, and insisted on it being repeated. His mind seemed more accustomed to the days when women had two or three 'really good gowns,' and even the assurance of Counsel that smart young women to-day would have many frocks without necessarily spending very vast sums did not do much to soften the impression that here was a woman who, like Habbakuk, was *capable de tout*.

Mary's friend, with whom she had been to the theatre, could not say what sort of frock Mary had been wearing, as she had kept her cloak on during the evening. It had been something dark, and that was all she knew. They had parted between eleven o'clock and eleven-fifteen on coming out of the theatre. She had understood Mary was going home, and had seen her drive off in her car.

Counsel then showed that a tab on the inner side of the frock bore the name of an extremely famous and extremely expensive Parisian firm. Even Mary's extravagance could hardly have led her to buy a frock from such a place. Moreover, a representative of the firm was summoned to say that they had never supplied Mrs. Spens; she was not one of their customers, and no account, even for one item, had passed through their books in her name. The price of the frock would have made it unlikely in the extreme that it had been paid for in any other way than by cheque. As to who had bought the frock, there the trail ended. For it had been dyed at some period, and it was not possible to say what the original colour had been, and, in consequence, the firm declared they could not trace it. The general effect of this evidence was to weaken the impression that had been made by the prosecution.

As to the shoes, Mary again denied entirely that they were hers, and, as they too proved to have been made and sold by a Parisian firm, and no purchase by her from them or any of their London agents could be traced, their identification as her property could not be made.

But when the question of tracing Mary's movements came up, her daily maid was called, and her evidence proved extremely important.

In her efforts to economize and pay off her debts, Mary had given up her two maids, and had done a great part of her own housework, with the help of a daily woman, Mrs. Hughes. During the all-important week-end, Jack Spens had been away from home. Mary was admittedly alone, and no evidence was forthcoming as to where she had been after she parted with her friend at the theatre. Actually, in view partly of her delicate physique, which rendered it difficult to believe the murder was her sole work, partly in view of Jack Spens' complete collapse, the police had at one time been inclined to suspect him of participation in the crime. Jack had, however, proved that he had gone to a friend in Norfolk for the entire week-end on the Broads, and his alibi was unbreakable. He had left on Friday morning and had not returned until Sunday night. Mrs. Hughes now stated that on the Saturday, the 8th, she had gone as usual at 8 A.M. to the Spens' house in Golders Green. She had let herself in with her key, and proceeded to do the kitchen and drawing-room and prepare the breakfast tray. She had not gone upstairs, for Mrs. Spens, when alone, always breakfasted in bed and did not like to be disturbed, and Mrs. Hughes was in the habit of going up with a tray at 9 o'clock. On that day she had been much surprised when, just before 8.45, she had seen Mary's little car drive up to the house. The front door bell had rung and, on going to the door, Mary herself had been there. Mary had explained that she had got up and gone to church and had forgotten her latch key, and Mrs. Hughes had unquestioningly accepted this, not having worked sufficiently long for Mary to know if this were likely or not. She had, however, noticed that Mrs. Spens was carrying a fur coat rather clumsily over her arm, and had been wearing a long black coat herself. She had been rather surprised at this, though the morning was unusually cold and dreary for the time of year. She had, however, not bothered herself particularly, thinking it was just a vagary of her employer. When Helen Bailey's mink and sable coat was produced and shown to her, she declared it was "the same sort of colour" as the one she had noticed over Mary's arm. On this point she speedily became confused, when cross-examined by Mary's counsel, and finally refused to be certain "one way or the other". She stated that Mary had only drunk a cup of tea, had run upstairs to her room for about ten minutes, and had then hurried out of the house, saying she had an appointment in town. Mrs. Hughes had left at 11 o'clock, and Mary was not then back. She was sure Mary had done no washing of any stockings or clothes while she was in the house; indeed, there had not been time. This was considered by Mary's supporters to be a point in her favour, for the silk stockings and shoes found in the wood had certainly been soaked with water, and presumably washed out.

Next, the housekeeper living in the house opposite to the entrance to "The Towers" was called. She stated that she had seen a car turn out of the Murray's drive at about 8.30 on the Saturday morning. It was a small closed car, resembling Mary's, but, beyond that, identification was not possible.

Mary's story of having gone to church could be neither verified or disproved. The church she said she had attended had a daily service, at eight o'clock, but as July 8th was not a festival or Saint's Day there seemed no reason why Mary, who was not in the habit of attending church except on Sundays, should have gone that morning. She had not been observed by any one.

The negative side of the defence has already been indicated. Denial that the frock and shoes were hers, denial that the footprints were hers, denial that she had been out of her own house except for going to church—all were persistent, but unconvincing.

As to any constructive defence, this resolved itself into an attempt to prove that some other person had had access to Helen's room, after the Friday evening, but here all attempts to prove anything were very doubtfully successful.

First the defence called Dr. Graham to swear that, when he was fetched to "The Towers" on the Monday evening, the carpet in the sitting room was still very damp. Dr. Graham stoutly maintained that this was so, and produced the notes he had written in his diary in support. Alan Murray, who rather weakened his evidence by his obvious desire to say anything possible in Mary's favour, also swore to noticing the damp look of the floor. Against this, the prosecution tried to establish the theory that a carpet which was thoroughly washed on a Friday would not have dried completely by Monday. But the defence pointed out that a fire had been lit in the room, presumably on the Friday evening, the day having been very damp and cold. The ashes showed that the fire had been well banked up and must have been burning with a good deal of heat for several hours. This evidence was, of course, intended to show that some person, who could not have been Mary Spens, had been in the room washing the floor subsequent to Friday night.

The other point brought forward was the finding of the bloodstains at the top of the inside of the cupboard door. Mary was so small that, were the marks made by her, she would have been reaching upwards to her fullest extent. It would have clearly been more natural, had she been the person in the cupboard, for her to hold by the panels of the door at a lower level. Further, as her counsel said, there was no conceivable reason why she should have pulled the door to from the inside if she only were in the room with the body. He drew the inference that some other person had been present, and, until that point had been dealt with, he asserted that Mary's guilt had not been sufficiently proved.

It was indeed on these few slender flaws in the case of the prosecution that Woods' mind dwelt. He could not rid himself of a latent feeling that all had not been discovered. He was oddly dissatisfied with the case built up against Mary, and he returned to court next day positively dreading the close of the proceedings, which he so clearly foresaw.

The judge, however, had none of Woods' misgivings. No summing-up could have been more entirely against the accused. Modern habits—including make-up, bridge and cocktails—seem by their nature abhorrent to those who dispense justice, and to create in their breasts a perfectly genuine belief in the total depravity of those addicted to them. It was hardly necessary for the judge to stress the points of the evidence against Mary—they were too striking already—but the tone of his remarks did subsequently call forth adverse criticism, so clearly did he betray his feelings as to the moral obliquity shown by this extravagant young woman, who admitted she had intended to abandon home and husband. But beyond a mild excitement at the stern and overwhelmingly unfavourable tone adopted, most of those present felt that no further thrills could be wrung from the proceedings, and indeed that the case as a whole had not proved 'one of the best!' There was, therefore, all the greater feeling of shock and excitement at the subsequent proceedings.

The jury retired and, after only forty-five minutes' deliberation, returned to court.

The Clerk, rising to his feet, asked of the Foreman:

"Gentlemen, what is your verdict?"

To which the Foreman, in the midst of a breathless hush, announced clearly:

"The jury are unanimously of the opinion that the prisoner is guilty."

Instantly all eyes turned to the prisoner in the dock, who, drawing a deep breath, cast an anxious glance at her counsel.

The Judge, leaning forward, put the usual question as to whether the prisoner had anything to say why judgment should not be pronounced against her.

At this point, the general stupefaction may be imagined when, instead of the pallid prisoner stammering out an inaudible protestation of innocence, her counsel rose to his feet and said:

"My lord, the prisoner wishes to make a statement before sentence is pronounced, either by her own lips or to be read by me for her."

To which the Judge replied sternly that the prisoner "was quite at liberty to make a statement, and to do so in any way she chose."

Whereupon counsel, having hurriedly whispered a word to Mary, and acting on her directions, then prepared to read aloud from a manuscript a statement clearly written out for this purpose beforehand.*

---

* If readers doubt the probability of this, they may be referred to the trial of Mrs. MacLachlan, where this actually occurred.

In a silence which was almost tangible, he prefaced the statement with a few brief remarks. He said that the prisoner at the bar had written out her story as to what had happened on the night of July 7th, immediately after her arrest. He, however, acting with her other advisors, had considered it advisable not to produce it at an earlier stage, but he now considered it his duty to yield to the urgent entreaties she had made to him that morning and to make her story public.

Chapter XI

THE STATEMENT

"Bring the villain forth"

Othello.

This was the story which Mary now told:

She had, for some months, been coming to the determination to leave her husband. Helen had, as Mary had already stated in her evidence, agreed to help her, and to give her some valuable pieces of jewellery so that she might raise enough money to live cheaply until she could support herself. She had not, however, taken the things with her on the Friday morning, as she had previously stated. Helen was busy, and anxious to get the household off to the country. They arranged, therefore, that Mary should come back later. As Jack and Eleanor Spens were old friends of the Murrays, Mary did not want to make trouble between the two families, and she and Helen agreed it was better none of the Murrays should know anything of her departure from her home, nor that Helen had helped her. They decided that Mary should come back without James Murray knowing she meant to do so. It was necessary that she should have the jewellery that day, for she wished to leave home on Saturday and find other quarters for herself before Jack came back on Sunday. As they anticipated James Murray would be at home all the afternoon and evening, they settled that the best—indeed the only time—would be after he was safely up in his room for the night. Mary was going to the theatre that evening, and would be driving herself home in her car. She could easily call in at "The Towers" on her way back. Old James always went up to his room at eleven o'clock, and his windows looked out on the garden. To avoid any possibility of his hearing the front door bell, Helen would be on the look-out, and would come down and let Mary in. This would be easy, as her rooms all looked on to the porch and front drive. She would be expecting Mary any time after 11 o'clock, and would come down to the door with the jewellery and the fur coat.

Mary had come home in her own little car, and had arrived at "The Towers" at 11.30. She had heard the big clock at the corner strike as she turned up the road. She had noticed, of course, the lights were on in Helen's room over the porch, as she expected. But she had been surprised to find the front door ajar—for this was so contrary to Mr. Murray's ways, and she wondered why Helen had so disregarded his well-known wishes. After waiting a minute or two, she had pushed open the door and gone in. She called Helen's name softly, and then went on up the stairs. The door into Helen's sitting-room was also ajar, but she heard some one moving inside. On going in, she found the room in darkness, but a light was shining in from the bedroom beyond. She went on through the bathroom and looked into the bedroom, but it seemed to be empty too. Fancying again she heard a sound behind her, she turned back to the sitting-room and out on to the landing, but there was no one there. She decided Helen must have been in her bedroom and would return there, so she decided to go in there and wait for her quietly, being afraid to move about the house for fear of disturbing Mr. Murray. But, on returning to the bedroom, and going right in, she saw, on going round the high tester of the bed, that the room was not empty as she had thought. Helen was lying on the ground on her back, undressed, with blood pouring from a terrible wound across her forehead and face and forming a great pool on the floor. Knowing that there were no maids in the house, she had not stopped to go and rouse old Mr. Murray but had set to work to do all she could for her friend. Throwing off her coat, she poured some water from the washstand jug into the basin, seized a sponge, sat down beside Helen, and, lifting her head and shoulders on to her own lap, began to bathe her face and head. At the touch of the cold water Helen had opened her eyes and gasped out "Mr. Murray did it." Mary had told her not to try and talk, and had continued to bathe the gaping wound until the flow of blood ceased. Helen, by now, was fully conscious. After a while, she wished to get into bed, and with Mary's help succeeded in doing so. The movement brought on fresh bleeding, and Mary had to bathe her thoroughly once more. She got the bleeding stopped finally, and a wet bandage put on. She washed away all the blood that had run down Helen's neck on to her chest. Helen had now revived enough to talk quite distinctly and was anxious to make Mary understand what had happened.

She told Mary that she had been in her room undressing when Mr. James Murray had come in. For some time he and she had carried on a liaison in secret. He was, in reality, her "admirer." Mr. Scott was only an invention to prevent the family from knowing. She had meant to break off the connexion, and had told him so that evening. He had been terribly angered at hearing this, and they had quarrelled furiously. He had lost all self-control and had snatched up the little battleaxe and struck at her. She had not known anything more until she recovered consciousness to find Mary bathing her head.

Mary could hardly believe this tale, and thought Helen must be delirious. She dared not cross-question her, for she was so weak from loss of blood. She wanted to fetch help, but Helen became too agitated at the thought of Mr. Murray being fetched, and there was nobody else in the house. Mary thought Helen should have some stimulant, so had at last got up and gone to the sitting-room to get some brandy, for she knew there was some in the cocktail cupboard. She had been startled on going into the sitting-room to find that the door of the big fixed cupboard, which she was sure had been shut when she passed through the room, was now standing open. Terrified at the idea that the murderer might still be in the house—for she did not believe Mr. Murray had done the deed—she had locked the door of the sitting-room on the inside. The bedroom door and bathroom doors were already locked. She had given Helen some brandy and had taken some herself, for she was feeling faint and sick with shock and fear. Helen had laid quietly in the bed, the bleeding from the wound had stopped, and Mary began to hope the injury was not so serious as it had appeared. She could not tell how time passed, but she thought it was about half an hour after Mary had first found her, which would bring the time to about midnight, that Helen began to complain of feeling very cold. Helped by Mary, she had struggled into the sitting-room, where there was still a good fire, and had laid down on the hearthrug with the pillows under her head and covered up by the eiderdown. Mary made up the fire again, and Helen seemed to doze off. Then a knock had come at the door, and Mr. Murray's voice, perfectly quiet and steady, begging Mary not to be frightened but to let him in. Helen did not rouse up, and seemed to be almost in a stupor. After some hesitation, Mary did open the door. James Murray had come in and began by imploring her not to be afraid. He seemed quite sober, but became very agitated, and Mary did not feel any apprehension or any fear either for herself or for Helen. He had, he said, never meant to hurt Helen but she had driven him beyond his powers of self-control and he had struck her in a brief moment of madness. He said he would do anything to help her, and to get it all hushed up. He went and fetched some hot water, and helped to bathe Helen's head. She again revived and spoke to him. He begged her to forgive him, and said if she would agree to say a burglar had attacked her, he would make it worth her while. He spoke of Glenda and Alan, and implored both Helen and Mary to shield him for their sakes. He had fetched more hot water in the basin, and had begun to try and clean the room—washing the stains and spots made on the floor where Helen had staggered in. In doing this, he had spilt the contents of the basin over Mary's feet, soaking her slippers and stockings. She took them off and put them to dry by the fire. Helen dozed off and on, but seemed to get worse, more restless, and more feeble as the night went on. James went in and out of the room. Mary sat beside Helen, watching her.

It was, she thought, after six o'clock when Mary grew alarmed, and told James they must ring up a doctor. James demurred, and said if the doctor came now "all would come out." Helen was not in command of herself and might not stick to the tale of a burglar. "It'll all come out," he kept repeating. Mary grew frantic, seeing Helen was rapidly getting worse, and said a doctor must come, whatever the consequences. She did not want to leave Helen, but she dared not risk further delay. To her eyes, Helen was obviously worse, and she had been expecting her to get better once the bleeding had stopped and she had slept. Feeling that Helen's life must be saved at all costs, and, finding that James still hesitated and was unwilling to go, she had at last jumped up to go herself. James had barred the way to the sitting-room door, so she had run through the bedroom, unlocking the door with the key, which was in the lock, and downstairs to go to the telephone. James came after her to the foot of the staircase, begging and imploring her to wait. He said Helen was very badly injured and no doctor could do anything. "I knew she was done for," he kept saying. He begged Mary to think of Glenda and Alan. Mary refused to listen and ran into the study where the telephone was. She shut and locked the door behind her for old Murray seemed so frantic she was afraid he would prevent her. She couldn't get any answer from the Exchange, and after wasting six or seven minutes decided time was too precious. She remembered Dr. Graham lived at the corner and meant to go for him. But, on running out from the front door on to the gravel drive, she realized she was bare-footed, and flew back to put on her slippers in order to run quicker. She remembered she had left them drying in front of the fire, so she rushed up into the sitting-room—and there was Helen, not as Mary had left her, covered up and lying on the pillow, but uncovered and lying on her face by the hearth, smothered in blood, and with fresh injuries to her head and neck. She was quite motionless—indeed she was dead. Mary shrieked aloud, and old Murray came rushing in. Mary felt utterly frozen with horror and fear. She could not move; felt she could not turn and try to run for her life; she could not defend herself, she could only gasp out "Don't kill me—don't, don't." Old Murray had at first seemed stupefied himself, then had told her to be quiet, he did not want to hurt *her*. He had tried to pacify her, and begged her to trust him and all would be well. He had repeated again and again "It was no good; I knew she'd die; I knew she'd die." He had taken Helen's body by the legs and dragged it into the bedroom. He had come back with water and begun to sponge the floor. Mary had refused to do anything. She had just sat in a chair feeling too sick and giddy to move or try to get away. James had told her to stop where she was, and had gone away and after a while come back with some tea, which he told her to drink. He had then brought her her stockings and slippers, which were now dry. They had gone down to the study. He had talked to her for a long time. He said, "Your life's in my hands, and mine's in yours." He had said he and Mary would both be thought guilty of Helen's death if the story came out, and pointed out to Mary she was covered with blood and could not prove her innocence. He said their only chance was to try and conceal their presence in the room, and to make the murder look as if it had been done by some one from outside. He had gone up and changed his bloodstained clothes. She had heard him moving about overhead in Helen's room, and, when he came down, he had told her he was washing away the blood, so as to leave as few traces as possible, hoping to make detection more difficult. He had suggested that she should write a note, one which should be supposed to be from Helen, saying she was called away for the night. He said this would give him a little more time to get the rooms cleaned up and his clothes destroyed. Otherwise, if he had to fetch the police at once, that very morning, it would be more difficult, and he could not so easily account for having heard nothing. If they could make it look as if the murder had been committed while he was out for his walk and not discovered for a day or two, it would all be much simpler, and he could deal better with the police.

Mary was so exhausted she could not argue and fell in with anything he liked to suggest. She could not think clearly, and only wanted to avoid opposing him and to get away. She had scribbled the words he dictated, trying to make her handwriting look like Helen's, and he had put the note up on the study mantelpiece. He asked Mary why she had come to the house, and she told him Helen had been going to give her some jewellery and furs to sell as she, Mary, was in desperate need of money.

Mary had refused to go upstairs again. Just as James came down finally, saying everything had been tidied upstairs, a bell had rung loudly. James had told her to stay in the study and had gone to investigate. He came back to say it had only been the milkman at the back door. Mary had been utterly terrified by the noise of the bell ringing through the house. She realized the horror of the position—she sitting there in her bloodstained clothes, and that ghastly corpse upstairs. She had tried to pull herself together, but could hardly take in what James was saying to her. He brought down the jewellery and Helen's mink coat. He told her she had better sell the jewellery as soon as ever she could. He advised her not to sell it all at one place. He told her where to go, and said she must give a false name and address. He advised her not to keep the coat, or any of Helen's things in her house, but to get rid of them, and her own stained clothes, without any delay. He had kept on impressing this upon her. He made her go into the lobby and wash and tidy. She had thrown off her coat on first finding Helen lying on the floor. She now put it on, and it covered her frock. Her slippers and stockings did not show, and she was going in her car, so hoped to escape notice. She felt better after this and able to go home. She went out, and the air helped to steady her. She had driven her car to her own home and she thought she had not met any one who recognized her. When she reached her house she found she had no key. She saw that Mrs. Hughes was in the house already, and looked at her watch. She put the car away in the garage, picked up the mink coat, for she dared not leave it in the car lest by any chance it should be found and traced. She vaguely felt she must hide it at once. She told Mrs. Hughes the story of having been to church and had hurried upstairs and put the coat into a cupboard and locked it. She had then gone as soon as she could to sell some of the jewellery. She took her own stained clothing as well, realizing she must at all costs get rid of it. She had felt so utterly exhausted on returning home as to be unable to think of any further efforts, and, realizing she must get Helen's coat and the pearl necklace out of her house, could think of nothing better than to take them to Eleanor's home. She knew Eleanor was to be away, and thought she would have time to evolve some way of getting rid of them before Eleanor's return. She dare not now leave Jack and her home, as she felt flight might somehow call attention to her and possibly arouse suspicion. She had not known of Eleanor's return on Saturday and had heard nothing of the footprints on the mat. The visit of the police had come as a terrible shock, but she determined to keep silent until she knew what James Murray would do. She saw that circumstances looked black against her, that she could not prove her statements, and that only a confession on the part of James could clear her. She waited confidently in the belief that, when he heard of her arrest he would come forward.

James Murray had sworn solemnly to her that if she were by any chance stopped on her way home and her bloodstained clothes noticed, or if in any way suspicion fell on her, he would then come forward and confess. She had believed he would keep his word, and had waited confidently for him to clear her. Even during the trial she had thought he would come forward when he saw how strong the case was against her. She realized he might be waiting—as she herself was—in the hope the jury would give her the benefit of the doubt and acquit her. It was only after the conclusion of the summing-up, when it was clear she had practically no chance of acquittal and she realized he meant to remain silent, that she decided she must speak out and, while declaring her own innocence, accuse James Murray of the crime.

*

The reading of the statement had taken a long time, but the court remained throughout it utterly still. When counsel came to the passage where Mary spoke of James Murray entering the room, all eyes turned to the seats where James and John sat together by Glenda and Alan. James himself remained apparently calm and immovable, but John Murray turned ghastly pale and seemed as if he would break out into protest.

At the conclusion all eyes were again riveted on the judge, and a subdued clamour of conversation broke out on all sides. No one could tell what would happen. Would the judge adjourn the case? Would he order the defence to proceed to prove the facts they alleged? Would he order a fresh trial? But the judge did none of these things. Speaking in what seemed exceptionally loud and harsh tones, he briefly dismissed the statement altogether. He considered it to be a mere tissue of lies, without any foundation in fact, and quite incapable of proof. Indeed he said that, in his experience, he "never knew an instance in which statements made by prisoners after conviction were anything else than in their substance falsehoods. A person who would commit such a crime as you have committed is quite capable of saying anything. And if such statements as we have now heard are to pass for truth with the authorities of this country there would be an end to the safety of the lives and characters of every man."

He declared that the statement conveyed nothing to his mind but the impression that it was "as wicked falsehoods as any to which I have ever listened," but that in any case he should be bound to act upon the evidence and verdict. He considered that Mary's attempt to incriminate James Murray—"a man of hitherto unblemished character"—was a wicked perversion of truth, made by an unscrupulous woman frantically trying to escape punishment for her crime, and to throw the blame upon an innocent man. He therefore proceeded to pronounce sentence, without further ado, and condemned her to death.

Mary had stood quite upright, listening to the judge's address. A bright crimson patch had come at each cheek as she heard his unmeasured condemnation of her statement, and realized the light in which she was now regarded. But the shrinking and shame which had seemed to bow her down during the trial had given place now to a greater firmness and dignity of demeanour. When the last words—"and may God have mercy on your soul"—ceased to echo through the court, she turned to leave the dock, but, as she did so, she exclaimed in clear, loud tones, perfectly audible to all:

"God will have mercy, for I am innocent."

It was felt by many of those who had listened spellbound to the final scene, as they began to struggle to get away and spread the thrilling news of this unexpected *dénouement*, that whether innocent or guilty, Mary had at least succeeded overwhelmingly in one respect—she had completely spoilt the judge's dramatic effect.

Chapter XII

THE CLUE

"Knock, knock, knock; who's there?"

Macbeth.

E arly next morning, Superintendent Gowing and Divisional Inspector Woods were conferring together. Superintendent Gowing was perfectly cheerful, for he had no objection to the glare of publicity. He felt that the police had done all that could be expected of them. They had found the woman who had been present at the murder; they had traced her movements; and produced the clothes she had so carefully hidden. Both jury and judge had agreed that Mary Spens was guilty, thereby endorsing the police view. Gowing saw no cause for dissatisfaction, and he was merely pleasantly excited at the turmoil in the Press.

Inspector Woods did not share this cheerful optimism. He had thoroughly disliked getting up the case against Mary, though he had done so with his usual conscientiousness. Yet he not only felt repugnance at the idea of a girl such as Mary, gentle, well-educated and beautiful, committing a crime of such brutality, but he found the attitude of the public perfectly odious. He resented the conviction, which experience had borne in upon him, that, in a big murder case, no real sympathy as a rule was felt for the murdered person, but that a desire to see some one caught, hounded down and sentenced to death was the chief excitement.

A similar situation to the one now created in the Murray case had never existed in England, though there was the record of a case of the kind in Scotland. Legally, the position was clear. The jury had found Mary Spens guilty, and the judge had condemned her to death. Her advisers would proceed to appeal. The question which now occupied the officials was that of investigating the assertions made in Mary's statement.

"It'll be interesting to see how the public takes this," said Gowing quite cheerfully. "From what I've heard myself already, it'll be a regular Dreyfus affair—half the world for her, and half for Mr. Murray."

"Well," replied Woods. "I've never really believed that we've got to the bottom of it all. I've always had a feeling there was some one else behind it and more evidence that we'd not turned up, and there are things in this statement which do appear to me to be true."

"Such as?" queried Gowing.

"Well, first of all, it's always worried me why the body had been washed, before the second attack. It didn't fit in with the actions of a single murderer, first, to strike her down, then to bathe the wounds, then have another go. Mrs. Spens' story does account for that, and quite convincingly to my mind.

"Then, I agreed with the defence as to the stains on Mrs. Spens' clothes. If she'd bent over that body and slashed away, the whole front of her dress *must* have been badly splashed with blood, to say the least. Whereas the skirt and slip were only stained below the waist and they weren't just splashed, they were soaked. That fits in again with her description of how she sat with her friend's head on her lap. Dr. Graham told us the first big wound must have bled profusely and for some time, and that would have produced the soaking of the skirt. Above all, to my mind, it accounts for those footmarks. That room had been tidied, and the floor in the bathroom and sitting-room both had been thoroughly washed over. No one doing that could have failed to see those footmarks. And if they'd not been left, we'd never have known a woman had been there. It looked too clear a sign for my taste."

"Do you think," inquired Gowing, "that Mr. Murray meant all along to implicate her?"

"Well, there again, that spilling the water over her legs and feet sounds fishy to me."

"You're assuming, of course," said Gowing dryly, "that her statement is true. You've got to remember what the judge thought; he'd no doubts at all it was nothing but lies from start to finish. Practically told her 'my good girl, no one can believe a word of your story'."

"Well," replied Woods slowly, "it's a cruel case which ever way you look at it. If she did it, and is trying to lay the blame on an innocent old man, she's as wicked as they're made, for all her gentle appearance, for, whether she gets off or not, this mud will stick to old Murray. Plenty of people are going to believe it against him. And then, if she's innocent and he's guilty, what an awful old devil he'd be—murder one poor woman and fix the blame on another. He'd be a bold man, too, for in that event he'd know the tale would be bound to be told in the end and might be proved against him."

"What about the cupboard?" put in Gowing. "You were always going on about the marks there. I suppose you think her statement proves he was hiding in there when she went in?"

"Yes," agreed Woods. "There again, we always knew some one went into that cupboard and pulled the door to behind them with their bloodstained hands—that's a certain *fact*. Of course, the prosecution meant us to think the girl was mad drunk and went wandering about the place in a frenzy and went in there herself. Possible, of course. On the other hand, if old Murray were there, he'd struck Helen Bailey down and left her unconscious, and must have believed and hoped she was dead. Then, if he heard Mrs. Spens enter the house, and tried to avoid her finding him, if he were hidden in the cupboard, he'd soon grasp that Mrs. Spens was bringing Helen Bailey round, and he'd soon hear her telling Mrs. Spens that it was he who'd attacked her. Well, he'd realize straight away the alternatives before him. If Helen Bailey lived, she'd be testifying against him, and his character would be gone and his life ruined. If she died, he'd now got Mrs. Spens to deal with. She'd have to be silenced somehow, either murdered herself, or bribed to hold her tongue, and that paved the way to more trouble in the future. Or, if he could but induce her to help him now, he might succeed in implicating her, and so make her harmless. It's a plausible explanation of what *might* have happened, and I must have a shot at seeing if I can verify any of her statements."

"Difficult to see how you'll do it," said Gowing, thoughtfully. "If you look at *motive*—well, each has a sufficient one. We know Mrs. Spens needed money desperately, and we know she sold that jewellery. We've both known cases where people, who'd been decent enough—up to then—have got led into stealing and from that into murder. Mr. Murray's is much the same position. If this story is true, he might kill from thwarted passion—that's not so uncommon—and then get led on into sacrificing Mrs. Spens to save himself. Possibly he might even persuade himself he owed it to his family—as Mrs. Spens had no one who cared much for her apparently, and no children to suffer.

"As to anything else, the only proof against him would be tracing any of his clothes that might be stained, or have been sent to be cleaned, or got rid of. That will, I should say, be precious difficult. He was alone in that house for three days, and had ample time to cover his traces. He had access to Miss Bailey's rooms, too, all that time, and could remove anything in the shape of letters which were likely to implicate him with her. I don't see where you're to find evidence, Inspector."

"I don't say I'll find it, but I mean to have a good look," replied Woods.

He spoke resolutely, for indeed the mental discomfort he had felt throughout the trial, intensified by the production of the statement, made him eager to settle his own doubts one way or the other.

"Don't be too ready to believe that statement," warned Gowing. "You've got to realize it's as the judge said—just her word—and a woman faced with the gallows won't stick at much. She's an intelligent girl, and she had time, too, remember. She knew the family, and the circumstances. She knew—was the only person outside the family who did know—that Miss Bailey and Mr. Murray were alone in the house. She had the week-end in which to think out a story—indeed, she had longer than that. Guilty people often produce plausible statements accusing some one else, and accounting in elaborate ways for things that tell against themselves. Remember she knew well enough the points she had to account for, and remember too she's only produced this tale when everything else has failed. You can't upset the verdict without something extraordinarily conclusive in the way of evidence."

"I know that, and I know she may be guilty, but I want to be more sure in my own mind than I am now," said Woods.

"Well," replied Gowing. "You get on with it. But I warn you there's going to be the devil of a row over it all."

I I

The Superintendent's forecast was actually an underestimate. The whole country appeared to go mad over the case. The "Murray

party" and the "Spens party" split families, broke friendships, ruined
the harmony of clubs. The Press took sides, even the clergy, and
every section of the public. Prejudice, of course, far outweighed
reason, and lovers of detective methods were overwhelmed and
shouted down by partisans of morality. Mary's shortcomings created
a host of violent enemies; her love of bridge, her extravagance, her
debts, and her avowed intention of deserting her husband, left not the
slightest doubt in the minds of a vast number that she was not only a
murderess but "a vindictive, lying, heartless wretch." On the other
hand, many young people, moved by animus against the old, as such,
never referred to James Murray in milder words than "that disgusting
old devil", and often in far stronger and more opprobrious terms. His
partisans, anxious to show he was physically incapable of the murder,
tried to stress his age, and supposed infirmities, one paper speaking of
him as "this mild, feeble old gentleman of fourscore years", a description which caused Alan and Glenda a sort of savage amusement.

A specially bitter controversy raged over the production of the
statement, and Mary's counsel was much criticized for having with-
held it till the end of the trial. He had consulted earnestly with her
solicitors over the best course to pursue. It was obvious that, if she
went back on what she first told the police and told her second true
story at the outset of the trial, she thereby admitted she had been
in the house, that she had practically witnessed Helen's death, and
that she had conspired with James Murray to conceal the truth. This
would make her liable to be charged as "accessory after the fact",
and actually lay her open to the death penalty. On the other hand,
if she denied having been at the house, and stuck to her original
story, there was a fair chance the jury might give her the benefit
of the doubt and acquit her. Actually her counsel himself, in his
heart, doubted the truth of her statement, and saw clearly that the
assertions it contained were incapable of proof. After much debate

it was decided that Mary's best hope lay in aiming at acquittal. As events proved, this course failed, and it then became imperative to produce her statement. No doubt if all had gone favourably for Mary, and the jury had found her "not guilty", her advisers would have been as warmly praised as they were now blamed.

While the Press and the public thus seethed and boiled, the position of the Murray family was deplorable. Rich, and hitherto respected, the whole affair had that nightmare quality which, in the presence of calamity, makes people say "this can't happen to *us*." Here was a murder, attracting the greatest possible notoriety, fixed upon a peaceable, quiet, respectable and wealthy family. It was awful enough to have Helen murdered; worse still when their friend Mary was accused. The climax seemed to be attained when James himself came under suspicion. The family was, of course, officially bound to support its head, and to take the line that Mary's accusations against him were utterly unfounded. James himself showed the fiercest animus against Mary. His was not the type to bear injuries with patience, or in silence. The violence and heat which flared up when he spoke of her, roused horrified revulsion in Glenda's heart. She had always feared and disliked her grandfather, and had for years known and loved Mary. Secretly she believed that, of the two, her grandfather was more capable of committing the crime than Mary, and her mind turned constantly to the tale which it was alleged Helen had gasped out in her dying moments. Was that story true? Had James in secret been Helen's admirer? Was it he who had given those presents? Could those two have carried on an intrigue under the eyes of the family? Such thoughts seemed inconceivably wicked, and the whole situation utterly alien to the peaceable, solid, middle-class standards of her life. Yet Glenda thought she knew Mary's disposition, and could not convince herself that Mary was capable of inventing such a story, even to save her life. It was impossible to discuss the case with her father, for John Murray had taken the affair terribly to heart. He was a changed person, silent, moody, and quite unapproachable. Alan was her chief standby, and between these two there was no need for any pretence or reticence. Finally, James, tired of the publicity and uproar, in strict accordance with his former way of life, issued an autocratic edict to the family. Mary was a vile woman; her name was not to be spoken; no reference whatever was to be made to the trial or to her pending appeal. No interviews, of course, were to be given to the Press. Neither Glenda nor Alan were to discuss the matter with any of their friends. No notice was to be taken of the deluge of letters which continued to descend upon the family—many of them anonymous. Everything was to go on as before the tragedy.

To Glenda, however, though she tried to obey her grandfather, the effort to dismiss the murder and the trial from her mind was futile. She could not help her thoughts continually dwelling on the problem. Talking it over with Alan, she put into words the ideas which tormented her:

"I can't help it, Alan. I do *know* Mary has always been honourable and kind. She never made any secret of her affairs. And I just can't believe she could have deceived everyone as to her whole nature. But Grandfather"—she stopped abruptly, for when it comes to the point hardly any one really enjoys saying out loud that they believe near relatives to be brutal murderers—"I'll tell you another odd thing," she went on abruptly, swerving away from the subject of James. "The police, of course, don't know Helen's character and ways. We *do*. And I'm sure if Helen had quarrelled with the giver, she would never have kept, or given away, that jewellery. She'd have sent it back. I don't believe *that* part of Mary's story."

Alan looked at her, and then said slowly:

"Well, you know that point struck me too, but it seemed to me to work just the other way. It corroborated Mary's tale to my mind."

"Why? How do you make that out?"

"Because I agree with you, Helen would have sent back those presents to the giver, if she'd been able to—but, suppose *Grandfather* had given them, how could she have given them back without all sorts of bother? That coat, how'd he then have got rid of it and all that? It's just because if *he* gave them it was impossibly difficult to return them that she might have given them to Mary. Don't you think?"

But Glenda again felt beyond her depths. She could not conceive such a situation, nor how it could have been dealt with, and could not bring herself to agree. She again changed the course of her thoughts: "Then, you know, what about that frock? I don't know for certain, of course, whether it was Mary's or not. She has so many. But all that about it coming from Paris was rubbish. She needn't have bought it in Paris or from the London shop at all."

"Do you mean it was given her? But Jack would have known, and there'd have been trouble over an expensive frock like that."

"No, I don't. But, you know, Mary wasn't altogether as extravagant as they made out. And she used to buy clothes sometimes from a lady's maid who sold all sorts of grand people's things. Mary may have bought this in that way."

"Mary worn second-hand things," said Alan incredulously. "Nonsense! I don't believe *that*. She'd never do such a thing."

Despite her unhappiness, Glenda smiled. "You don't know much more about women's ways than the judge," she said. "Lots of girls who haven't big allowances, and who want to be really smart, do that. They can get absolutely lovely model clothes, which have only been worn once or twice, for next to nothing. I know Mary used to do it, and I was surprised it didn't come out at the trial. Of course, it was much better for her that it shouldn't—and I can just imagine how the judge would have glared and doubted his own ears and all that."

Both were silent for a while, thinking how sad it was that trifles which seemed to be so harmless and unimportant in everyday life could have such a vital influence in swaying opinion, even if ever so little yet so cruelly, against a human being when on trial for their life. Mary's faults had seemed so negligible, yet now they were proving terribly heavy in the scales when weighed against her.

"I'll tell you one thing that really does worry me, Glenda," Alan said meditatively, "and that is the change in Father—it's positively startling."

Glenda looked at her brother apprehensively. "Yes," she said slowly, "he *is* changed. He's not a bit like he used to be. He's so unhappy and restless, and looks ill."

"I should think he does. I know the people at the office notice it—and yet I don't see why he should take all this to heart so terribly, beastly as it is."

"Well, you know," hesitated Glenda. "I think perhaps he was fonder of Helen than we quite knew. I know once or twice I caught him looking at her in rather a special sort of way—indeed, Alan, to tell you the truth, it did just cross my mind once that perhaps he thought of asking her to marry him."

"Well, we shouldn't have minded having Helen as a step-mother, if she'd suited Father. I often think he's had rather a rotten life, you know. But I wasn't myself thinking of anything of that sort." He paused; then went on, "No, it's what's going on between him and Grandfather that bothers me."

Glenda made no answer, but her anxiety seemed to deepen.

"It's like this," continued the young man. "Father's never one to talk, and he's never discussed Grandfather, or his position in the business, with me. But lately I can't help knowing they've not got on—and Father's being the aggressive one."

"What on earth do you mean by that?"

"I mean what I say. Father goes out of his way to make trouble with Grandfather. Once or twice lately I've had to go into their private room, and I've heard Father talking in a way that absolutely took me aback. They've been really rowing, and Father was the one who seemed to be taking a strong line and insisting on his own way. And his whole manner to Grandfather has changed. He shows he dislikes him, and he doesn't see more of him than can be helped."

Glenda sighed. "Of course I've never known how Father managed to put up with things all these years. I suppose he knew Grandfather owned the business, and was the most competent person in it."

"Don't you believe that. Father's done all the real work for a long time past. Grandfather's been a figure-head, and just pottered in and out and given himself a little occupation. But Father's never seemed to bother about that sort of thing—and now it isn't even the business part that's the trouble, as far as I can see. It's more as if he'd a personal animus against Grandfather—and just when, in one way, you'd expect any one as decent as Father to stand by the old man—whatever he may think in his heart," he added, rather appalled at the implications of what he was saying.

Glenda looked rather distressed. "It is really, all too horrible for words, Alan," and her voice trembled. "I don't know what's to become of us. It is such misery to go on like this—and yet I suppose Father would never feel we *could* desert Grandfather at this point and go off to Red Barns, and have a little peace there, away from this hateful house and the memory of it all."

"No more we could," said Alan shortly. "We've got to stick together, whatever we think or feel." He was, in fact, repenting already that he had said anything to his sister. He had only upset her, and, incidentally, himself, by dragging out into the light of day thoughts which, so far, he had barely acknowledged to himself.

"We've got to stick it out," he repeated. "And personally I'm thankful that Grandfather seems fairly well disposed and isn't always down on me as he used to be. At least there's that amount of consolation," and, with that, he got up and went away, feeling that the conversation had gone quite far enough, and that his grandfather was wise in tabooing discussion of the subject at all.

III

Others besides Glenda pondered these aspects of the statement relative to Helen Bailey and old Mr. Murray and saw the implications behind James Murray's alleged appearance in Helen's room. Inspector Woods found himself perpetually balancing the probabilities between the two versions of the crime. He drew up for himself a table showing the pros and cons for each party. James Murray had an excellent character, held a high position as head of a flourishing business, was an important householder, and had been universally respected. Mary Spens had an equally good social position, but she had against her the disadvantage of her extravagance and her quarrels with her husband. She had not, in the general eye, as good a record as Murray. Setting aside the question as to relative trustworthiness, Woods next had to consider the inherent probabilities in favour of the accuracy of the statement. Mary had produced a tale which fitted in extraordinarily well with the various facts which had been brought out at the trial. Here, of course, it became important to find out at what stage she had drawn up her statement. If it had been written out during the course of the trial, she would then have known exactly what she must account for, and could invent a tale accordingly. However, on interviewing her solicitors and counsel, it was shown conclusively that she had sent for her solicitor while she was under arrest before the trial began and had dictated to him the whole story. Her statement was therefore in existence, and legally attested, before ever the trial came on. She had made it when ignorant what evidence would be produced, and what allegations she would have to meet.

Woods pondered deeply over this. If she were guilty, she had been extraordinarily clever. She had, in that case, seen the importance of, and attempted to account for, the stains on her clothes, the bare footprints, the washing of the body, the finger-marks on the glasses, the stains in the cupboard. Yet, it was perfectly possible for a clever and unscrupulous woman, desperately trying to meet the case against her, to reconstruct the scene of the crime mentally, a scene which, if guilty, would be impressed upon her brain, and bit by bit evolve a story to meet the facts.

Yet here Woods found his own secret prepossessions influencing him. His mind really refused to believe Mary either could or did plan out such a tale, clearing herself at the expense of the dead woman's reputation, ruining the honour of the Murrays, and endeavouring to bring old James Murray to the gallows instead of herself.

"No," he exclaimed aloud. "I just don't believe that hypothesis really fits in with this crime and this woman."

The other alternative then lay before him. Was James Murray the murderer? Had he so contrived matters as to obliterate the traces of his own presence and to leave those which implicated Mary Spens?

Again Woods went over the facts. He saw that Mary's story could only be proved if certain points could be substantiated.

First, according to her version, the crime had been committed not before 7 P.M., as James Murray would have them believe, but much later, at about 11 P.M. Could this be verified? At once Woods saw that the only hope lay in the chance of some person having called at the house after 7 o'clock, who might have heard voices or the sound of a quarrel, or possibly some one, such as the postman, might have been delivering letters and noticed Helen Bailey in her room. He set to work at once on this point. Hitherto, no efforts had been made to find persons going to the house after 7 o'clock, for the truth of James Murray's time-table had never been doubted. Woods found himself wishing Mary's advisers had notified the police of her statement earlier in the proceedings. Much precious time had now been lost, and it would be far more difficult to verify facts now, when weeks had gone by and when memories were overlaid by the details and immense publicity given to the trial.

Indeed, at the end of a couple of days, Woods had made no progress. Every tradesman who might have been making a late delivery at "The Towers" was traced and interviewed. None of them had called after three o'clock on the Friday afternoon. Woods had hoped the laundry-man might have called late, but to his great disappointment found "The Towers" got their laundry returned on a Thursday. The last postal delivery was made at 9.30, and the man on the round was interviewed. He stated that he had, he supposed, delivered letters at "The Towers" that evening, but he had not noticed anything. Pressed as to whether there had been lights in the rooms over the porch, he was quite unable to say. "He had not noticed one way or the other." So Woods advanced no further in that direction.

Failing the establishment of the hour at which the murder was committed, there yet remained other possibilities to be followed up. If Mary were to be believed, then James and Helen had been carrying on an intrigue. Confirmation of that would certainly change the face of the situation, for it would supply a motive for James committing such a crime, and it would prove Mary to be telling the truth on one of the most hotly contested points at issue. Was it possible for Woods to discover any facts which would prove whether there had been any liaison between James and Helen? Here he was baffled at once. The most careful search of Helen's papers and belongings had yielded no sort of clue. Now he obtained permission to go through Mr. Murray's, but he knew in advance he would find nothing there. As to the jewellery, it had either never been in cases with a maker's name or those cases had been destroyed. Publicity brought no response from any firm which might have sold either the necklace, watch or ear-rings. If James were the donor, he had covered his traces, or possibly bought the things on one of the occasional trips he still made to the Continent. In vain did the Inspector rack his brains in the endeavour to find some point where this part of Mary's story could be either corroborated, or definitely proved untrue. He began to despair, yet all the while, there in Mary's statement, unperceived either by her counsel, or by herself, or by the Inspector, lay one little piece of information which might prove the touch-stone Woods so eagerly sought. The credit of discovery was to be given to the Superintendent, who had worried himself far less over the case than the impressionable Woods, but who, none the less, had also gone over the statement carefully.

One morning Woods received an urgent summons to Gowing's office. On entering he found his chief busily jotting down some notes, with an air of subdued excitement.

"Look here, Woods," he said, glancing up. "I've realized something we ought both to have noticed before this in that statement—indeed, I can't think how it came to escape us."

"What's that?" said Woods, rather taken aback.

"The point about the milkman," replied Gowing briefly.

"The milkman?"

"Why, yes. Look here. We know it was proved that Mrs. Spens did not return to her own home until 9.45 A.M. on Saturday. The case for the Crown rested on the assumption that she spent that night at 'The Towers,' at first concealing herself in the locked room while Mr. Murray was about, and then attempting to get rid of the traces of her presence, and not leaving until she could do so without attracting attention in the morning."

"Yes," said Woods.

"Mrs. Hughes' evidence showed that she did not go home until 8.45. The caretaker at the house next to 'The Towers' actually saw a car, resembling hers, go past at 8.30. The postman, making the early delivery at 7, had seen a car, answering the description of Mrs. Spens', in the drive. Those facts, taken in conjunction, were held by the Crown to prove that Mrs. Spens was out of her house all night. They drew the conclusion, of course, that she spent the time at 'The Towers' in doing all that washing and cleaning. She couldn't prove she'd been at home, and she didn't really convince any one by her story of getting up early and going to church. The Crown certainly maintained she was at 'The Towers' until 8.30 A.M."

Woods nodded agreement. Gowing went on:

"That's just what's so important, and yet we never saw where that would lead us if her statement were true. See here—Mrs. Spens stated that while she was, as she now admits, at 'The Towers' talking to Mr. Murray in the early morning and preparing to leave, the milkman called—at about 7.15. If you remember, she said that she was so terrified by his ring at the bell that she turned absolutely faint and ill, and could not go home for a while. She stated that Mr. Murray went to answer the bell, and told her it was the milkman. That can be definitely proved or disproved. The milkman would have his round, at a certain time, and surely he would notice anything so unusual as the owner of a house like 'The Towers,' and a man of Mr. Murray's type and reputation and way of life, opening the back door to take in the morning milk?

"In addition, he may have observed Mr. Murray's clothes. Assuming the statement to be true, were those clothes stained, or had he changed them? Can we get anything there?"

"He'd changed them," said Woods at once. "Mrs. Spens said he changed in the very early morning, after tidying the room, and I suppose he put on the same sort of suit he'd been wearing. But I'll tell you what, Superintendent," he went on, with growing excitement. "If Mr. Murray *did* open the door to the milkman at 7.15, that would prove he was up and about before Mrs. Spens left the house. If that were so, how could she have got downstairs, and out of the house, and driven her car away without his seeing? She'd left her car a bit down the drive, she said, but he'd have been bound to see it or hear it. The engine would be stone-cold and take a lot of starting up and make a lot of noise. She'd never have got away without his knowledge. Why, this milkman may settle the whole case! How on earth came I not to notice it!"

"And another point," said Gowing, with growing interest, bordering indeed on enthusiasm. "How does he account otherwise for being up and dressed so early? What should he be doing about the house fully dressed at that hour? If everything were above board, he'd not have got himself up and fully dressed by 7.15. I think we're really on the track of something here, Woods!"

But the Inspector, the first surprise over, now began to feel some doubts. "Of course, these milkmen have a big round, and it's pretty well two months ago now. The man may not remember who opened the door to him that day, and he's got, for our purpose, to be sure it was Saturday, July 8th, and no other subsequent day. Remember, sir, Mr. Murray was alone until after Monday morning, and might have spoken to the man on Sunday or on Monday as well. He'll have some story to account more or less reasonably for his being up and about so early, even if he is deceiving us. I'm afraid, too, that his clothes won't help us; whether he'd changed or not, they'd be all alike to the man at the door. I expect he'd done the thing thoroughly while he was about it and changed into something suitable."

"But," said the Superintendent, "if he *did* change his clothes, where are the stained ones? Woods, we'll be in trouble over this; half the press already says we ought to have been more suspicious. We should have checked Mr. Murray's clothes more carefully. If one of his suits is gone, where and how did it go? I wish we'd paid more attention to him."

"And been no further on," retorted Woods. "You forget, sir, that, if Murray is the guilty person, he was alone in that house from Friday to Monday. The weather was very cold and wet, and we know he'd a fire every evening. He could burn anything he wanted easily enough."

"True," answered Gowing, "but I think we must make more sure of all that. You see, if any of his suits do prove to be missing, that's an indication for us to probe a bit deeper. We might try to find out, too, if any suit-case or portmanteau has been taken away. There are three distinct lines we must follow up: the milkman, Mr. Murray's clothes, and the possible removal of any parcel or luggage from his house."

"Very well," replied Woods. "I'll set all that going, sir, and we can but hope to get on to something."

"And don't concern yourself too much about the public agitation," added Gowing. "That we must expect, and put up with, in a case of this sort. It may help us in a way, for, with so much notoriety, any one concerned in the case will find their actions noticed and reported upon in a way that wouldn't otherwise be possible."

"That's true," replied Woods, rather gloomily. "But I'd rather have less publicity and more certainty we're on the right track myself."

Chapter XIII

THE PURSUIT

"Let us meet, and question this most bloody
piece of work, To know it further"

Macbeth.

T hree days later the two sat again in the office, this time both looking perceptibly more harassed. Well they might, for the excitement and uproar in the Press and amongst the public were indescribable. Petitions were being got up on behalf of Mary Spens, and meetings held, and these were met by counter-blasts from the "Murrayites." All sides agreed in demanding further activities on the part of the police. Yet, as Woods confessed, he could get no further evidence. Those who believed in the statement were redoubling their activities on Mary's behalf, as time grew short.

James Murray's family had been asked to swear to his clothes. But so autocratic had he always been that his family had never concerned themselves with his personal attire. The dead woman had been responsible for seeing that his suits went at stated intervals to be cleaned and repaired by a valeting service. She also had seen to the replacing of worn-out garments. The maids were completely vague as to the number of his shirts, or pairs of socks, or the number of his pairs of boots and shoes. As to his suits, he invariably wore the old-fashioned business man's dark coat and dark striped trousers, one suit exactly resembling another, and nobody could be positive as to the number. The parlour-maid had at first said she believed he had "three or four," but, pressed repeatedly to say exactly if it were three or if it were four, she became muddled and contradictory, and Woods saw that accuracy on such a vital point was hopeless to expect from her. Yet, without accuracy, he could get no further.

Again, all efforts to trace the letters Helen had received from 'Mr. Scott of Bournemouth' proved futile. Glenda and Alan had known her to receive letters, said to be from Mr. Scott, but could only say they were typewritten. Neither had ever had one of the envelopes through their hands, so nothing definite could be obtained as to postmarks.

The police saw clearly enough that, were the statement true, and had any sort of love affair existed between Helen and James, such facts as there were could be fitted into that hypothesis. Both were clever enough to have devised a scheme of corresponding under the very eyes of the family, when necessary. Both were frequently alone in the house, when Glenda and Alan were away, and John Murray at business. James usually went to the office three or four days a week, but otherwise he was much at home. Helen's habit of shutting herself in her rooms every afternoon, with the alleged intention of writing to her arthritic admirer, might have been devised to cover a less innocent occupation.

Such implications, of course, were cheerfully made by the 'anti-Murray' faction, in private, for nobody was foolish enough to risk an action for defamation of character which James Murray was ready enough to bring if opportunity offered. Indeed, were he innocent, he was to be pitied, for enough suspicion had been aroused to make only very tried friends anxious to be on good terms with such a notorious family. "The ruin of an innocent, God-fearing man" was indeed made the subject of a passionate plea issued by one of the 'Murrayite' papers to Mary Spens, urging her to confess and make reparation for the ill she had done.

The new phase of the mystery, upon which it had entered after the publication of Mary's statement, had of course called into play all the activities of those who interest themselves in crime and mystery. Inspector Woods was deeply irritated by the innumerable letters he received offering him advice and 'solutions' of his problem, but many a home was cheered and invigorated by the interest universally taken in such a baffling affair.

Alan Murray, who, as the date for hearing the appeal approached, found it hopeless to try and go to his work, and far too trying to go to his club, so great was the excitement, now seemed to derive a grim sort of satisfaction from discussing the whole matter with complete cynicism. He felt that another week or two ought to see the matter settled, and yet dreaded the final end for Mary.

"I'll tell you what it is, Glenda," he said. "I've come to the conclusion that there are three solutions to choose from: (1) Grandfather is innocent of the whole thing; or (2) he contrived the whole thing, did the murder, and arranged for the blame to fall on Mary; or (3) Mary is lying to shield some one else, some one whom she knows did the murder."

"No, that's perfectly impossible," objected Glenda. "In these days no one would shield another person like that. Mary wouldn't try to do so at the expense of Grandfather, if she knew he were innocent. That she'd never do. Either Mary is lying from start to finish or Grandfather is; you can't get away from that."

"Well, in either case, life is going to be unbearable. Half the people I used to know avoid me like the plague now. I might have done the murder myself. And how is it going to end? Either with Mary being hanged one of these mornings, just when we are getting up for breakfast, or, if by any chance she's reprieved, then half the world will always think Grandfather was guilty—and probably add that we all knew, and shielded him."

"It's no good you talking like that. You said yourself we'd all got to stick together."

"I know I did, but this waiting about is too awful. Once it's settled—the appeal I mean—I do hope and trust Father will put his foot down and let us all go off abroad for a bit." He spoke bitterly, and with cause, for, as each week passed, a barrier seemed to be rising round the Murrays, cutting them off from the world of ordinary humanity.

"It's like the plague," said Glenda. "I just feel as if I were a leper. No one *wants* to be with us, only a few people think it's a moral duty."

One of those who did feel it a duty was Eleanor Spens. All that was best in her rather hard nature seemed to have been called forth by the catastrophe. Jack still remained ill, shattered by the calamity, and quite unfit to be up and about. He stayed in bed, thankful to be forbidden to see any one. Eleanor, involved as she was in the case, showed great self-control.

"My dear," she said to Glenda. "I don't mean to talk about it at all. I believed it to be my bounden duty to tell the police of that suitcase. And of course, you know what I feel and believe about Mary. But I have made a resolution I will not mention her name"—and this she kept. She had stepped into the gap left by Helen, and proved of the greatest practical help. She had engaged fresh maids for the Murrays, Glenda's rather feeble efforts having been unsuccessful, for their former staff neither wished to stay, nor did James Murray, in his violent moods, wish to keep them. She had even supervised all the funeral arrangements, and seen to the cleaning of Helen's rooms before they were shut up, for no one could bear to go into them, nor was there any one to use them. She restored some semblance of outward comfort to the household. Above all, she took over the task of bridging the gulf which separated James Murray from the others. John Murray clearly found it impossible to resume his former deferential, rather subdued relations with his father. A sort of defiance, not quite angry, nor quite contemptuous, seemed to tinge his attitude. It was easily seen that, at best, he resented the scandal; at worst, he actually doubted his father's innocence. Morose and silent, he was not often at home, usually going now to his country house and travelling up every day. Glenda and Alan were, however, bidden by him to remain at Highstead, and, to their surprise, for, as Mary's friends, they had thoroughly disliked her enemy, they found themselves positively glad of Eleanor's frequent visits. She helped to make their formal meals less ghastly, talking to one or other, and she would actually go with James to his study and presumably entertain him there, for her voice could be heard talking away cheerfully, with occasional deep interjections from him.

"In fact," remarked Alan. "It's the old platitude—Adversity shows your true friends—but I never thought we could have liked Eleanor so well."

"You see," said Glenda. "She *has* her good side, but I suppose she couldn't help hating Mary just because she loved Jack and saw Mary didn't make him happy, and that brought out her worst part."

Meanwhile, time passed, and at length the day came when Mary's appeal came up. The only new evidence brought forward dealt with the question of the milk round. The milkman had proved illusive. The man on the round was indeed forthcoming, but he had a boy assistant, and, in the case of a big house like "The Towers," the man was in the habit of remaining himself at the gate with the cart and sending the boy round by the back-drive to the back-door. The boy on that round had left since July 8th, and great efforts were made to trace him. At last, the very day before the appeal, Woods succeeded. A boy of about sixteen presented himself, explaining that he had been in an isolation hospital for diphtheria and had not heard of the hue-and-cry after him. He was a boy with no home, living in lodgings which he changed frequently, and his landlady had no idea that he was the milkboy so anxiously sought for.

Woods listened impatiently to these explanations, longing for the boy to come to the point and tell the story of the morning of the 8th July. When at last he did, however, Woods was rewarded. John Rawlings, for that was his name, perfectly recollected the day, for it was the last one on which he was at work. The next day, Sunday, his throat had felt so sore that he had stayed at home, and his landlady was able to corroborate the date. He was equally sure that the door had been opened by "old Murray." Young Rawlings had been very surprised to see the master of the house, but he knew the maids were going away, though he had vaguely thought some one else would have been got in. He was positive that it had been not later than seven o'clock, for he always checked the time taken on that round by the tower clock at the corner of the next road. The rounds were worked on a schedule, and punctuality was important. He was prepared, in short, to swear that on Saturday, July 8th, the door was answered by Mr. James Murray at 7 a.m. Mr. Murray had said no milk was wanted and none would be wanted until Tuesday. It was shown that, in fact, he had breakfasted at his club on each of the three days, Saturday, Sunday, and Monday.

When the appeal was heard, this new evidence was produced, and the now famous milkboy told his story. James, examined on this new point, seemed to have been aged by his recent experiences and anxieties. He was muddled and confused, and showed difficulty in answering the questions put to him. 'Anti-Murrayites,' of course, declared this only part of his clever scheme to pose as a decrepit old fellow incapable of crime. The gist of his answers was the reiteration that he "had no recollection" of the matter at all, but, *if* he did go and open the door at 7 a.m., he was sure he had got up so early on account of his worrying over Helen. It was proved he always got up at eight, and had been known in summer to get up earlier on occasion. As to saying no milk was needed till Tuesday, that was natural, for Helen's note said she would be away for the week-end, and the family would not be back till Tuesday.

A new question then arose as to the door having been locked. Young Rawlings was sure it had not been fastened, that the 'old man,' as he called Murray, had just come and turned the handle and opened it. He had been kept waiting some minutes after ringing the bell and was standing on the step, and was certain there had been no turning of the key or undoing of the bolts. This was of importance, for, if Rawlings were right, and the key not turned in the lock, then it followed that the door was open at 7 A.M., and it at once became clear that some one might have gone out that way. Mary, it had always been clear, must have left by the front door, as her car had been in the front drive. John Murray swore that, when he tried all the doors on the Monday evening after the murder had been discovered, the back-door had been locked and bolted on the inside. James professed no recollection of locking or bolting it, and merely reiterated he "could not remember anything whatever." There lay the impasse. Was young Rawlings right, or was it simply an error of recollection on his part, after so many weeks had gone by, during which he had been extremely ill? If he were right, then that door had been opened during the night and was, in fact, neither bolted nor locked at 7 A.M. and must have been re-locked and bolted subsequent to that hour.

The truth seemed impossible to come at, and its importance cut both ways. On the one hand, it might mean that old Murray had been up and about before 7 A.M., and in that case must have seen Mary, who was proved not to have left the house before 8.30, and to have had her car with her in the front drive. On the other, it might mean that Mary herself had opened the door; had, for some unknown reason, gone down the back-drive and up again to the front for her car, and had, of course, not been able to lock and bolt the door behind her, and that Murray had quite unconsciously done both some time during the early morning. The daily woman had not arrived at the house until half-past nine, when she had been let in by Mr. Murray. The back door was then locked, she was sure.

Then fresh excitement was caused by a further statement put forward by the milkboy. He now declared that, on going up the drive with the milk bottles in their wire basket, and while waiting at the door, he had noticed quite fresh traces of a motor car. It had rained during the night and then cleared, and marks would be visible on the damp gravel. It was not usual for cars to go up to the back door, the way being extremely narrow and inconvenient for turning. The tradespeople habitually left their cars and vans in the road, and ran up the narrow passage on foot. It was, however, actually just possible for a car to pass up, and Rawlings now produced this tale of having seen the tracks of one.

This simply had the effect of casting doubt on his previous statements. Everyone thought that he was carried away by the desire for notoriety and the wish to be dramatic. Why had no word been heard of this car before? Why had he waited until the theory that some one might have escaped by that door had been propounded? No, Rawlings' fresh evidence was not helpful to Mary, and was not given much credence. Her appeal was, in fact, dismissed, and the original verdict of 'Guilty' therefore held good. The eternal argument then appeared in the Press—'Should a woman hang?' But before very much could be done in the way of organizing fresh petitions on this score, the Home Secretary settled the matter. The death penalty was remitted, and Mary received instead a life sentence, which, of course, only commended itself to a few reasonable—or indifferent—persons. The partisans on either side remained totally unappeased. Either Mary was innocent, and should not have been punished at all, or she was guilty and should have been hanged. Either Murray was deeply injured and maligned, or he should have swung for the murder. As it was, Mary lived, though most uncomfortably, and James Murray found existence very far from the agreeable, pleasant state which, his adherents maintained, was his just due. He went off for a holiday to the seaside, but, being recognized there, found himself unpopular, the small boys of the place going so far as to boo him in the streets. He defied this persecution as long as he could but, in the end, reluctantly cut short his stay and returned to the seclusion of his own house. There he shut himself up grimly, leaving John to manage the business, occupying himself as best he could, and only going out on Sundays to the parish church.

Glenda and Alan were frankly miserable, but, as they had foreseen, their grandfather entirely refused to consider going abroad, or leaving the house for a year or two, and they were obliged to make the best of an odious situation.

It seemed that the case must remain for ever the subject of dissension, and that the truth as to the events of that horrible night would never be known. The irony of the situation lay in the fact that both James Murray and Mary Spens did know exactly what had occurred—the truth lay either with one or the other of those two. One of them was lying, but the innocent and the guilty alike could not prove which that was, and the general public could only decide in favour of one or other, according to its predilections.

II

Altogether, from everyone's point of view, it was an unsatisfactory case. Inspector Woods felt it to be so more keenly than most, for, apart from being the officer actually engaged upon the case, he found his subconscious self perpetually gnawing away at him. He could not forget the girl now in jail and the old man still in that now haunted house. Finally, in despair, he decided that his work was really being affected by his constant preoccupation with the matter, and he determined to make one further effort to settle his mind, failing which he actually contemplated resignation. Accordingly, he once more sought Superintendent Gowing, who, however, proved unwilling to reopen the matter with him.

"We can't get any further, Woods, and we ought to consider it all closed," he said. "Look here: these are the facts, those that are proved and known:—Mrs. Spens was present in the house; she made those footprints; she took the jewellery and the coat. Mr. Murray was in the house; he did, I consider, open the door to the milkboy at seven; that door was then already locked. Nothing more is known or can be proved. Then, points not cleared up, but of interest: The car which young Rawlings says had been up the back drive; the question of Mr. Murray's clothes; the question as to who was Miss Bailey's admirer—not enough there to be worth wasting any more thought over. We can't get any more evidence."

Woods sighed. "Yet, you know, I feel it's like being out in a fog; if only I could get one gleam of light, I believe I could find the way. I shall wait just one more month, Superintendent, and then I'll give up detective work and take to market gardening."

But before the time was up the gleam came, and, as in real fogs, showed the Inspector something totally unexpected.

It was now nearly a month since the appeal had been dismissed. Woods was in his office when the telephone rang.

"Hullo! Inspector Woods speaking."

"Ah! Mr. Woods," replied a man's voice. "I'm afraid you'll think I'm worrying you over nothing, but I should like a few minutes' talk with you."

"Name, please, and on what business?" snapped Woods, who considered persons ringing up an inspector should be more businesslike.

"Oh, I am the Registrar of Marriages for Paddersmith, and I have a communication to make with regard to some persons in whom I believe you have been interested. I can't, of course, give names on the telephone."

Woods felt a vague quickening of interest. "If you can come along at one o'clock, I can arrange to give you a few moments then, in my own time."

"Right," and the Registrar rang off.

At one o'clock he was shown into Woods' office, and remained with him for ten minutes. At the end of that time, Woods showed him out, and as the two stood talking for a moment or two in the outer office, Riley, who was entering up some records there, caught some of their conversation:

"Well, of course, it's all unofficial, Inspector, and everything may be perfectly normal and above-board. But I confess I did recollect the law of evidence relating to husband and wife—and I thought it all rather a curious coincidence. In short, I found myself wishing several times that your attention should be drawn to my notice-board, and finally I decided just to point it out to you myself, before, maybe, it was too late—but strictly unofficially, you know, strictly unofficially."

"Quite, quite," said Woods reassuringly. "It's an interesting bit of information, and, of course, might have come to our knowledge in many other ways."

The Registrar, fussing amiably, now got himself out of the room, but turned back again to say:

"And you realize the names have been on my board for the requisite ten days, so any time now will do?"

"Yes, yes," replied Woods, "and I'm very much obliged to you for your news."

Finally, the visitor having got himself down the steps, Woods came hurrying back. He snatched up his hat and rushed out of the office. A couple of hours later, he came back, and at once sent for Riley.

"Well, Riley," he began jubilantly. "I hardly dare believe it, but I've an idea we may get the light we needed on that Murray mystery. There's something in the wind here that seems to me suspicious. It's made me think we've got some one else to deal with, and perhaps we'll get more now from trying a fresh angle of approach.

"It may be all correct and above-board, but I'm going to follow my instinct and believe the contrary. I'm going to assume there's something being hidden from us here and make a fresh dash at it."

Riley looked completely mystified. "I gathered there's a marriage in the wind, sir, but what can a marriage have to do with the Murray case?"

"Well, you know, Mr. Spens got himself out of a nasty situation by claiming the husband's right not to give evidence against his wife. I think that's put an idea into some one else's head, and it's certainly put it into mine. But now, Riley, we're on terribly uncertain ground. We mustn't make a mistake, there's been too much fuss and trouble in the Press already over this case, and we've been hauled over the coals quite enough as it is. We must go warily, and I'm not going to tell even you just what I'm after for the moment. Time enough, if I find I get enough to act upon.

"Now, as a sort of indication to me that I'm on the right track at last, I want you to look up that Rawlings boy again."

"Don't think he'll prove very helpful, sir," said Riley. "He turned sulky when the public laughed at him and his motor-car tracks. He'll not be any too anxious to help us again more than he's obliged."

"Well, be as tactful as you can, and smooth him down, for it's just over that motor-car business I want him. I'd nothing then to enable me to carry the matter any further, but now—always supposing this new light isn't a will-o'-the-wisp—I've something to connect up with. Tell him we're not in the same boat as the public or the Press. Tell him we always looked on him as our most important witness, and all that. Get him ready to do his best, and then take him up to this garage"—here the Inspector wrote some directions on a pad—"ask the owner to run you out the car I've specified, and then get Rawlings to look at the tracks it makes."

A light dawned on Riley's face. "Oh! you think there had been another car up there that night after all, and you've an idea whose car it might be?"

"Well, that is just what I *have* got—an idea, and nothing more yet. But it's an idea that leads on to others. Anyway, to come down to facts, I tell you, Riley, I do suspect an individual, and I've had one piece of good luck. This individual—and I won't tell you yet who it is—has a car with a special feature as regards the tyres. If Rawlings is really the smart boy he seemed to be, he'll have noticed that peculiarity, and he'll recognize it now, and that'll encourage me to go a bit further with my speculations."

"Rawlings said nothing at the appeal about any special features of that track," said Riley gloomily. "Nothing of that sort came out."

"No, I know that," said Woods testily, "but he got so pounced on and ridiculed directly he began to say he'd seen those tyre-marks, that he just shut up. He'd enough sense to know that, if he'd said there was something distinctive about the track of one tyre, why he'd just have been the more laughed at and the less believed—they'd have said he kept on going one better each time—first the door—then the car—then the marked tyre. No! I don't think the fact that he said nothing at the time was conclusive. Don't, of course, prompt him—just show him two or three tracks, including the ones made by this car I've picked out, and see what his reactions are."

"Right," said Riley, and off he went, thoroughly intrigued by this new development. When he returned and presented himself in Woods' office, his expression showed at once that he had obtained some results.

"Yes," he said, in response to Woods' unspoken query. "He came along with us. We got out four cars and ran them along a piece of soft road up in the neighbourhood, as you'd suggested. We got the tracks good and clear. Rawlings went at once to those made by your special car, and said straight off, 'Those are the tracks like the ones I saw up the back drive at The Towers.'" We all asked him what made him say that, and he showed us that the marks of one of the tyres was quite a distinct type, and, of course, there it was on the special car—a different sort of tyre. It must be some sort of foreign make. I've sent our motor expert along, and he'll look at the car and identify the make of the tyre, and we'll verify where it was bought and all that."

"Yes," said Woods softly. "That's a great help. We know now that that car was up there on that night."

"*We* may know," retorted Riley sourly, "but Rawlings' evidence wasn't taken much account of before and won't be now."

"Maybe not," returned Woods placidly, "but I'm not relying on young Rawlings. I've something more up my sleeve yet, Sergeant. I've only taken Rawlings and the motor-car as corroboration for my own personal satisfaction. He's a weak link, but he is a link, and now I'm going on to see whether I can't forge something a good deal stronger in the chain I've begun."

He spoke with unwonted cheerfulness and certainty, which caused Riley to look at him rather wonderingly. The Inspector's alacrity sprang from practical certainty coming from the sudden resolving of all inward doubts and waverings. Woods had made up his mind at last. He believed he knew who was guilty and how the murder had come about and what had lain behind it all the time, and, his mind once settled, he was determined to act on his belief at all hazards to himself and his career. Accordingly, within the hour, he was down at the Yard, seeking an interview with Superintendent Gowing, putting before him briefly but clearly—for he was now a convinced man—his new views and explaining the action he was preparing to take. The Superintendent was aghast and showed it.

"But you've no proofs, man, no proofs whatever. This is all mere supposition and surmise, and based on what's probably all innocent and correct."

"I know, sir," replied Woods doggedly, "but I feel I must risk it. I know if I'm wrong, if this is a perfectly innocent affair—well, I shall have made a bad mistake and there'll be trouble for me, and I'll have to pay the penalty—dismissal, perhaps, instead of resignation. But I tell you this: I've got the whole affair on my nerves. I can't sleep properly for the ideas that come into my head; I can't settle to my routine jobs; I feel I'm not working as I should, and this new scheme will settle it one way or the other. I've made up my own mind, and I couldn't go on now without acting on what's my absolute conviction."

"But what do you propose to do? You can't take any steps to prevent this marriage—it's legal, and you've no power to stop it."

"Well, sir. I'd like a warrant ready, and I'll be prepared to serve it myself and stop the wedding for a time, even if that's all I do. I'm going to run it very fine, but Riley here will watch the house and, directly they've started for the Register Office, he'll go in with Colburn and Wilson and two more and comb the place at top speed. It's all I can do, but I believe myself it'll work. If I'm right, they'll find what they'll be told to look for, and I think I'll even be right as to the place where they'll find it. Riley will telephone to me, at the Registrar's private office, where I shall be waiting. If he's in time I'll make the arrest there and then. I reckon we'll do it, and, if we don't, why, I'll take the consequences."

"Even if you're right—and it'll be a miracle if you are—you're not done with it. You'll still have a good deal of evidence to get together," mused the Superintendent, impressed despite himself by Woods' confidence and readiness to risk his whole career on one throw."

"I'll chance that," said Woods grimly. "I think perhaps it'll come easier than we think, once we know we're on the right track now."

"If indeed we are," said Gowing, still rather doubtful. "It's a terrible leap to take—but you seem to have set your mind on it and, in any case, I believe I agree with you. We must take the chance, for it's the very last we shall have, and I do feel there's something there which will never come to light if this marriage goes through. If you're right now, and we do nothing it'll be hopeless in the future."

"Quite, and I couldn't ever rest to think the case hadn't been finally settled. I'd sooner be kicked out of the Force," and, with that, Woods went off. He felt perfectly composed, perfectly confident. He believed that, for once, fate was putting into his hands the choice between risk and safety, and he had no hesitation whatever—he meant to put fortune to the test.

A day passed and nothing occurred, but, on the following morning, the anxiously expected telephone message came through to Woods. He unlocked his private drawer, took out some papers, and looked in for a moment on the Superintendent. Something in his face, a grim jubilation and suppressed excitement, spoke for him.

"H'm—off to the wedding?" observed the Superintendent, trying to repress the slight thrill he felt.

Woods nodded. "An hour now will see it settled," he said. "But I know I'm right."

Exactly an hour later in fact, he, with great outward composure, arrested Mr. James Murray and Miss Eleanor Spens as they entered the Register Office, preparatory, as they had mistakenly believed, to their marriage.

Chapter XIV

THE TRUTH

"All shall taste the cup of their deservings"

King Lear.

Money was at the bottom of it all," said Woods in a calm, reflective voice. After a week's incessant activity, he was taking an afternoon off, and had gone in to supper with his uncle, who had expressed a strong desire to go through the particulars of the notorious case and hear it from the inside. The trial of James Murray and Eleanor Spens had been concluded, and they had been found guilty and condemned. No petitions were got up on behalf of either, for the second trial impressed on the imagination of the public the callous wickedness with which these two had murdered one woman and endeavoured to get another hanged for their crime.

"Money?" queried Uncle James.

"Yes," said Woods. "It all began—and indeed ended—with that. If old Murray had had enough money, none of this would ever have happened." He settled down to tell the whole story comfortably and at leisure.

"To begin at the beginning, we find the origin of the whole affair in what had been slowly simmering in that family for some while past. Helen Bailey was a woman with a great deal of character. She knew her own mind and she knew what she wanted. She'd led her own life, and she'd kept her own counsel. It suited her to have a good, quiet, respectable home behind her, like 'The Towers.' So she stayed on there, first as governess, and then as housekeeper. She'd strong feelings, too—of various kinds—and she was genuinely fond of the young people there. She was fond of Mary Spens as well—there was no pretence about all that. But she knew well enough that time was passing. She'd had ample experience of her attraction for men, but I daresay she felt it might begin to wane, or perhaps she thought a better opportunity to settle down comfortably wasn't likely to come her way. Anyhow, whatever her motives, she entered upon a liaison with James Murray. The two of them took great precautions to keep the matter secret. Helen Bailey, of course, wanted to keep her reputation, and I think, too, she genuinely wanted to retain the affection and respect of the young people. Her feeling for them was part of the better side of her nature, and we don't know what had driven her into her relations with men. So she insisted on the invention of 'Mr. Scott,' which effectually prevented any suspicion arising on the part of Glenda, Alan, and Mary. She could, in this way, accept James Murray's handsome presents, and make any plans that were necessary. I've found out since that she actually joined him abroad once or twice, when the Murrays believed her to be on her holiday at Bournemouth. It was on these trips she chose the pieces of jewellery."

"How did you get to know all this?" queried Mr. Simpson. "She left no papers, and he never confessed to anything, did he?"

"Not he—but his son did. John Murray came and had it all out with me—after the—er—funerals," said Woods rather awkwardly. "He'd had an awful time, and I was sorrier for him than I've often been for any one. He'd had a terrible part to play, and his life and business are both pretty well spoilt now, through no fault of his own."

"How did *he* know?"

"Helen had told him," said Woods curtly, "and showed him a letter or two she'd kept, and other things as well. She'd meant, if she found it worth while, to marry old James. All old Murray's outward life of severity and self-restraint had been, as is sometimes the case, the means he used to try and conceal—for it proved he had not been able to control, his passionate and coarse nature. There had never been any open scandal, but once at least, as his lawyer informed John after old James' death, he had been obliged to pay out hush-money. As he grew older, of course he found it more difficult to manage his affairs as he wished. Helen Bailey gave him what he wanted, and he grew more and more dependent upon her. Gradually he came to see that he wanted to make his hold on her more permanent, and she, in her turn, began to contemplate marriage with him as a way of providing for her future. James was close on seventy: she was forty. And I suppose she thought she'd have long enough as a wealthy widow to put up with him for a few years as a husband. Then she suddenly realized that John Murray wanted to marry her too. He'd been attracted long before, but he was no fool, and he had his ideas about Helen. I think he came to suspect his father was keen on her, though he had no idea of the true identity of 'Mr. Scott,' and that brought him to the point. Helen was honest enough in some ways, and, when he asked her to marry him, she told him the truth, and said she was practically engaged to marry his father. It was a fearful blow to John, and made him understand how strongly he felt. It didn't set him against her; it only made him realize how much he wanted her. He begged her to give up James and marry him instead. He promised to keep her secret. She told him she didn't care for the old man, and admitted she preferred John, but said she'd the future to think of; she was tired of poverty and couldn't face the prospect of old age. If she threw over James now, he'd be beside himself with disappointment and rage—for she'd led him on, and she'd the power to rouse men— and he'd turn John out of the business, so it was no good thinking marriage with him would compensate her in the least for the loss of James' wealth.

"Then John opened her eyes for her. James wasn't wealthy any longer. He was so autocratic he had managed the business in his own ways and they were not modern ways. He'd got into difficulties and even, in his efforts to save himself, into shady actions, and been forced to admit it to John. John had advanced money out of capital inherited from his grandfather to save a scandal, and, in return, had acquired the chief share in the control of the business and a hold over his father. In addition, he told Helen what old James had carefully kept from her and which proved vital in causing her to throw over old James. His mother, James' first wife, had left a very large fortune, invested in trust securities, on which 'The Towers' was largely kept up. It was settled on John himself, her only child. James had a life-interest in it, but, if he remarried, it would go straight to John. James, having now lost most of his own fortune, was almost completely dependent on his wife's money. That was the reason why James had remained a widower, for, as John knew perfectly well, he would have been only too anxious to take another wife before this, had it not meant forfeiture of a large and secure income. He was of that outwardly severe and harsh type which considers women as inferior beings and yet conceals, beneath a rude contempt, very crude and passionate desires. Helen had exercised too powerful a fascination over him and he had now resolved to marry her at all costs. He had perhaps trusted that, in view of her long association with the family, John would accept the situation and allow his father to enjoy the use of the first Mrs. Murray's fortune. Of John's own feelings towards Helen he was entirely ignorant. He was crafty enough to keep the whole financial situation from Helen herself.

"This revelation of the financial position had completely altered Helen's plans. She tried at first to break with James without committing herself. Finding her unexpectedly drawing back and raising difficulties, James, as might have been foreseen, simply became more pressing and more importunate. He began to lose his self-control, and some very unpleasant scenes took place. Helen had tried to return him his presents, but he utterly refused to accept them, and told her if she persisted he would make a scandal. He threatened her with declaring openly that she had been his mistress, and Helen realized, to her angry disgust, that she would find it rather an awkward accusation to rebut, and one which would effectually ruin her future.

"John Murray believed that, at the fatal week-end, James had meant to try and force Helen into a promise of marriage. Looking back, he had realized how extraordinary it was for James to be willing to be left without proper servants in the house, and he remembered how the suggestion had come from him that a daily woman would suffice. No one can tell now what he intended.

"So much for what I learnt through John Murray as to the early part of the affair. Then, to come to the murder itself. When I'd heard the 'statement' read in court, and after I'd considered it well, and decided it was probably true, I reconstructed the crime in the light of that account, and I got an idea as to the sequence of events. The murder then seemed to me to fit in and form part of a series of happenings, all connected with the relations existing between Mr. Murray and Miss Bailey. Clearly Mrs. Spens had only become involved through an accident. Yet, being so involved, her evidence was of the greatest importance, for the dead woman had, before she died, told her how the attack upon her had come about.

"I believed Mrs. Spens had told us the truth but that she had not told the whole of what she knew. Nor, indeed, had she. When Helen Bailey lay with her head on Mary Spens' lap she had managed to tell her the whole story, not only of her intrigue with James Murray but of her decision to marry his son John, and had declared this was the true cause of James' violent rage and of his attack on her. Mary Spens suppressed this, even in her statement, for with pathetic loyalty she still wished to spare the young Murrays, and even John himself, from avoidable suffering. Now that John Murray has made the early story of the quarrel clear to me, I have got Mrs. Spens to give me the complete version. So we actually have, as it were from the lips of the murdered woman herself, the account of all that happened, and we can reconstruct from the beginning the story of what actually passed in that house during that night.

"This, then, is the tale told by Helen Bailey herself. Late in the evening, when she believed he had gone to his own quarters, old Mr. Murray had suddenly appeared in her room. He was, of course, unaware of the fact that she was waiting up in expectation of a visit from Mary. He had begun to urge her once more to marry him, and had gone on to threaten her. Weary of his importunities, anxious to get rid of him, and snatching at the chance of stopping him once and for all, Helen in her turn had rather lost her self-control and her prudence. She had turned violently upon him, and had accused him of deceiving her over his money affairs. She had told him defiantly that she now intended to marry, not him, but his son, John; that John knew the whole story, but was prepared to overlook her past history and to make her his wife. She added that John would protect her now from possible injury, and that James could do nothing against her or against John. James had burst out furiously, and declared he would ruin the two of them. She had tauntingly answered that, on the contrary, his ruin lay in the hands of his son. She revealed that she knew all about James' financial misdemeanours, and that she and John intended to use this power to force James to accept their marriage and his own humiliation. The loss of this woman, the realization that the son whom he had always despised—even for his generosity in shielding him and allowing him to retain his position in the business—had actually known how to exercise self-restraint and to bide his time, proved altogether too much. James must have seen in one blinding flash that the life of authority and secret self-indulgence was passing from him for ever. He saw that he would lose everything which, to him, made life worth living, and that both authority and the woman would pass to his son. Mad with fury and mortification, possibly feeling at least he would see this woman did not triumph, he struck her down.

"Up to this point in the story," said Woods, "we had really known a good many of the facts, and I had suspected more. We knew Helen Bailey had been attacked when she was expecting Mrs. Spens. I, personally, believed the 'statement'. I saw that, if it had been Mr. Murray who struck the first blow, he fitted in with all I could reconstruct of the crime. He was in the house; he was familiar with Miss Bailey's ways; even his height fitted those marks on the door of the cupboard. I saw, too, how well the hypothesis that he was 'Mr. Scott' fitted the facts. If 'Mr. Scott' had been a real person, I was quite positive we should have come upon traces of him, and that he or his relations would have come forward by now. There had been nothing discreditable, as far as could be seen, in the story of his admiration and friendship for Miss Bailey. His non-appearance was, to my mind, inexplicable. But if 'Mr. Scott' were 'Mr. Murray', everything fell into place.

"Beyond that point, however, I got into further difficulties. Mrs. Spens' story told us of the first attack, and of her absence during the second one. Now, as I kept turning it all over and over in my mind, I was always confronted with the problem as to what James Murray had done with his suit of clothes and his boots. I knew well enough how great would be his difficulties in getting rid of them. I knew, from investigation, that nothing had been destroyed or concealed on the premises. Everything had been searched with a view to finding any such traces. I also knew, from the experience of Mrs. Spens and her action in trying to get rid of her own incriminating garments, that these missing clothes ought to bring me evidence of guilt. I didn't see that anything else would. When all my efforts finally convinced me that no trace could be found—and remember I was inwardly certain James *had* struck those blows, and that those blood-soaked clothes *must* have existed—I fell back on the old axiom: Never accept an impossibility, but assume that what seems unlikely may be true. I knew those clothes were not on the premises, and could not have been destroyed without trace. Therefore I was bound to assume James had conveyed them away and hidden them. I cross-examined his daily woman, and the chauffeur who drove him into town each day, most carefully, and I satisfied myself he had never left the house with any parcel or suit-case during that week-end. I found on each occasion when he did leave the house he had gone straight to his club, and, again, the porters there assured me carrying nothing. Yet, on the Monday night, those clothes had absolutely disappeared. I was left with the improbable but possible fact that some one else had been at 'The Towers' on the Friday night and had removed them."

Uncle James, absorbed in this reasoning, nodded acquiescence.

"There I stuck," continued Woods. I thought of every possible person. I suspected Mr. John Murray, I even thought of young Alan, but I soon found that John, young Alan, and Miss Glenda had, beyond doubt, spent the whole of that week-end down at Lewes. I did not see any way of getting further light. It must either have been some very intimate and close friend of James—and he had none that I could hear of—or some one who became accidentally involved.

"Then, again, I could never be satisfied as to that second attack. I could not see why, if Miss Bailey had revived and been on the mend, matters shouldn't have been arranged, as Mrs. Spens told us they

were, and a story fixed up as to the assault having been made by a
burglar. If the 'statement' were true, Mrs. Spens had gone down
to ring up a doctor, leaving Miss Bailey pretty well unconscious.
There was no great risk of her ever recovering enough to betray
Mr. Murray to the doctor. I couldn't visualize the old man going
back to the unconscious woman and repeating the attack, only this
time so much more savagely. It struck me as needing more explanation than we'd got. Nor need he have feared that Mrs. Spens
would burst out with the true version to the doctor. I was pretty
confident she would never, if it could have been avoided, have given
Mr. Murray away. She'd have kept to the story of the burglar. The
way she kept silence until the very end of the trial convinced me of
that. Helen Bailey couldn't, in the state in which she was described
to have been, even if the doctor proved successful in reviving her,
have given any very coherent account, much less one to justify a
man of Mr. Murray's standing being accused of murder. No, I had
a conviction that second attack wasn't accounted for by the facts as
we knew them. James Murray wasn't in danger enough to repeat
his first assault. Then it occurred to me that perhaps the solution
lay there. The second person, of whose presence I was becoming
suspicious, might have been responsible for the final attack. I realized
that Mrs. Spens never saw Mr. Murray in the room with Miss Bailey
after she herself had run downstairs. He'd followed her, and stayed
pleading and arguing with her. He'd only come in *after* she'd gone
back, as far as what she'd actually *seen* went, and the expression in
her statement was 'he seemed perfectly stupefied'. That gave me
an inkling. Had that 'second person' been near at hand, gone into
Helen's room while he and Mrs. Spens were downstairs, and made
the final assault? I only guessed, I had no proof, and, try as I could,
none came."

"Go on," said Uncle James, much thrilled by this account.

"Then came the discovery of the milkboy. That gave me the first confirmation of my theories. I saw that the tracks of the motor car were, in all probability, those of the 'second person'. But Rawlings' evidence did not carry the conviction to others which it brought to me. No one believed in his tale, and actually it carried me no further. I had no idea whether the 'second person' were a man or a woman. I had no sort of clue to their identity, much less to that of their car. I was forced to abandon my efforts. I could only hope that perhaps chance might give me the hint I needed. If only I could get some suggestion as to the person I sought, I could then try to identify their car and trace their movements."

Chapter XV

THE REASON

"I did wish her dead"

Richard II.

H e paused, then, after a brief interval, went on rather slowly. "Actually, the complete story, from the standpoint of the different individuals concerned, of what did happen in that fatal night has all been put together now. I've had one most interesting experience. The mentality of the person who keeps a truly intimate diary has always puzzled me, but I've never before personally come across a concrete example. My theory, when I read such diaries, has been that they were the expression of a frustrated life—these individuals have poured out on paper just the secrets of their own souls, just what they kept hidden from their associates. I'd always believed, too, that they were usually persons of strong individuality, who, all the more, were able to repress and conceal their feelings and thoughts from the world around. Eleanor Spens proved to be one of these individuals, luckily for me.

"What I'm going to tell you now comes from a diary we found in Eleanor Spens' house. It was put away in amongst a lot of her books, bound up like one of a set, with false titles printed on the backs. She was one of those people who keep an absolutely intimate diary, a record of her feelings as well as of her actions. She'd sense enough to know locked drawers call attention to themselves, and people will take trouble to find out what's in those drawers, and will read a book that's obviously meant to be private. She had more brains than most, or perhaps I should say brains that led her to act differently from most people. So she'd used a set of old, shabby, bound manuscript books, that had come to her from some great aunt, with a title stamped on the back 'Tour to Naples 1860–1', and there they were, standing in her shelves, and there I found them after her arrest. The last two volumes were her diary, not her old aunt's. She'd taken other precautions—used a shorthand of her own, as many people do, but our experts decoded it soon enough. And she'd never put the real names or places. You might quite well have thought it all an attempt at novel writing, until you'd our special knowledge of the true interpretation to be put on some of the incidents. If you remember, Dr. Pritchard kept a diary too—and put down all the events of his various murders as they occurred, but the glosses he added covered up their true significance until he too was found out. Well, this diary was rather in the same style. It wasn't used or produced at the second trial because it wasn't necessary. We'd proof enough without, but it fills up gaps and tells us how it all looked and happened to this other woman. So here we actually had from Eleanor the true version of what had gone before the arrival of Mary Spens on the scene—events of which Mary herself was quite unaware.

"Mary had thought she'd come in immediately after the assault on Helen. She was led to think that because she only derived her knowledge from what Helen told her. Helen herself didn't know what had happened while she lay unconscious. But Eleanor Spens did, and her diary made it all plain. This is what had happened:

"When, in the climax of his rage and disappointment, James Murray slashed at Helen Bailey with all his strength, and thought with triumph he'd prevented her from casting him off—well, at that very moment Nemesis did really overtake him, for Eleanor Spens walked into the room.

"Her diary describes how and why she came to be there at that particular moment. You'll have understood already how much of this crime turns on personalities. These people had no ordinary motive for this murder; they were led into it, partly by circumstances, partly by faults in themselves which they hadn't succeeded in conquering. Old Murray went all wrong because he couldn't achieve an ordinary, happy, settled married life. Eleanor Spens went wrong because she'd not got the better of the fault which was the curse of her life—jealousy—that's to say her natural affections all turned and twisted into evil. Her diary relates that when the night of the 7th July came, it found Eleanor in a fearful state of overwrought nerves. She had been through a great deal that day. When Mary had rushed away from her own home after breakfast, she had told Jack she meant to leave him and she knew Helen Bailey would help her. Jack at once telephoned to Eleanor to tell her his version of the quarrel, and both had agreed that Helen could not do much for Mary. Eleanor, however, had wondered to herself whether old Mr. Murray might take Mary's part. She had noticed, in her bitter jealousy in everything concerning her sister-in-law, the special friendliness James showed to the girl whom Eleanor felt deserved no such kindness. She longed for Mary to leave Jack, but she wanted her to be poor and friendless, not supported and helped by a rich and devoted family. She realized, moreover, that Mary's departure would mean Jack's return to her, Eleanor. All day she had wondered restlessly what had been decided, what had Mary arranged with Helen. She had herself intended to go away that week-end, meaning to spend it in Brighton, and Mary knew of her intention. She had therefore driven herself down in the afternoon, hoping to find distraction from her anxiety. After dining alone, she suddenly decided the suspense was unbearable. She felt she must know what Mary had done and what arrangement she had made with Helen or old Murray. She got out her car and drove up to Town. She went to Mary's house but found no one there, Mary being actually at the theatre. Determined not to go home without the knowledge she wished for, she decided to call round by 'The Towers' and try to find out from Helen what was settled. She did not want to see James Murray, and as it was late feared to disturb him. So, leaving her car at the back she had walked up the drive, trusting to see by the lights in Helen's room whether she was still up. As she reached the house, she saw the lights were on in the rooms over the porch. To her surprise, she found the front door open. James told her later that, having determined to bring matters to a head, he had walked about outside, waiting to see the light go up in Helen's bedroom. When he did see it spring up, he had hurried in, had not, in his excitement, waited to put the chain on, and had forgotten to let down the latch.

"Eleanor, after hesitating on the front door step, had heard loud, angry voices coming from the rooms above her head. She could tell there was a violent quarrel going on, and, as the man's voice rose, storming and threatening, she had decided to go in. She had run upstairs, and, as she did so, heard a loud, terrible scream, followed by the sound of a heavy fall. Rushing into the room she saw Helen prostrate, bleeding from a great gash across her forehead, with James standing stupidly over her, the weapon in his hand.

"Eleanor had not dared to go near and touch the body. She was sure the wound had been fatal. She had not liked Helen; she felt no special horror on her behalf; she simply felt this was an appalling catastrophe to happen to an old friend like James Murray, and she tried to think what could be done to remedy it. While they were both standing there, James still dazed and Eleanor endeavouring to keep calm and yet rouse him to a sense of the position and get him to explain, if he could, why he had done this, they had both heard a car come up the drive and stop at the door, and, almost before they realized what was happening, they heard some one enter the hall and call softly 'Helen'. Eleanor tried to open the bedroom door, but it was locked, and she dared not wait a moment to try and unlock it, for fear of meeting the newcomer face to face. Seizing James by the arm, she had hurried him through the bathroom and into the sitting-room, only to realize that whoever was in the house was nearing the top of the stairs and must soon come face to face with them. Frantically, she pulled open the door of the big cupboard and dragged James in besides her. The cupboard would scarcely hold them both, and James had come sufficiently to his senses with this new peril to try to pull the door shut upon them, thus leaving with his bloodstained fingers the marks which had been so inexplicable to the police.

"There they had remained for a few moments, not daring to move as long as there was the risk of Mary turning back into the room. They expected every moment she would rush out to give the alarm. Then, to their horror, they heard Helen's feeble, hoarse tones, and her first words betrayed what James had done. Realizing that Mary was now fully occupied with the injured woman, they had crept out, had listened until they were sure that Helen was indeed telling the story of the attack, then, going down to the study, they had begun to consider what could be done. Both saw that all turned on the nature of Helen's injuries. Old Murray was sure she could not recover. 'I know she's done for,' he kept repeating. Eleanor was steadied by the need for planning, and, roused into active partisanship by the fact that Mary, whom she hated, was involved, pointed out that, if Helen were to die, and before she could tell any one else, it would only be necessary to bribe or terrify Mary into silence. She had made no other suggestion—though," said Woods significantly, "I'm not sure whether left to herself, she might not have fallen back on a simpler and more certain way of silencing her. James, however, had always been fond of Mary, and he believed he could induce her, for the sake of her long-standing friendship with the whole family, not to betray him. If Helen lived, he thought both of them would fairly easily be brought to keep silence, and some tale of a burglar must be concocted. Helen would not want the story of her liaison to come out—Mary would have no special reason to ruin the happiness of her best friends.

"The idea of a burglar roused another train of thought in Eleanor's mind. She had wondered if Mary would attempt to get a doctor, and knew that, if so, Mary would naturally come down to the telephone. At all costs, no doctor must be summoned at this stage. So, slipping back to her car, she had fetched some strong tweezers and had cut through the telephone connexion. Nor was this done any too soon, for movements overhead and the murmur of voices coming through the floor made both of them fear that Helen was reviving. James, now composed and perfectly master of himself, had therefore gone upstairs and into Helen's room. Eleanor, in whose brain hatred of Mary, acting on her own violent excitement, had made all sorts of vague ideas ferment, went into the empty room opposite to Helen's door and tried to focus her thoughts. The shock of the night's events had completely driven all restraint and all memories of her own decent, orderly life out of her brain. She began to go over the situation in her mind. She knew Mary was there alone with the dying woman; that she had come there secretly late at night; that Mary was the only person who could betray the true story. Vaguely she felt that, if the worst happened and Helen died, there might be a possibility of fastening the guilt of the crime upon the girl she hated so violently. After some long time, during which she allowed these vile thoughts to take possession of her mind, she heard fresh sounds and, looking out, saw Mary come hastily out of the bedroom opposite, her frock soaked with blood, her whole face wild and distraught. The sight had somehow pushed the hesitating Eleanor over the verge. She felt her brain echoing with the words 'Any one would believe she was the murderess'. She saw James hasten down after Mary, gathered from this that Helen was worse and Mary wanting to fetch a doctor. She heard him arguing and beseeching Mary below. Before her brain had time to cool, before she could restrain the devilish flame of hatred which seemed to burn through her, she ran into the bedroom and, snatching up in her turn the weapon thrown on the hearth by James, she began to slash wildly at the almost delirious Helen, on fire with the determination to make an end, and resolved to fasten the guilt on Mary. In vain had Helen feebly tried to roll over, or to protect herself from the pitiless rain of blows. Lost to everything, Eleanor only stopped when she realized Helen had ceased to move. And, at that moment, she had heard James Murray begin to re-ascend the stairs. Eleanor went out to meet him and, only pausing to listen, said briefly 'It's done—it's over'. She went back to the empty room to try and still her now shaking limbs. For a long time she sat there in the darkness, hearing the voices of James and Mary, but paying no attention. James had finally come in search of her, and bade her go and wash herself in his bathroom. He told her quite briefly that he had settled with Mary, who had promised not to betray him, for, of course, she had never suspected Eleanor's presence. He was his old, grim, self-reliant self, and had told Eleanor that Mary would not dare to tell, she was much too deeply implicated herself. He had gone off and changed his own clothes and made himself tidy. Finally, Eleanor had crept out at the back, while he was still occupied with Mary, being of course obliged to leave the back door unlocked. Her suit-case was in the car. She had got in and changed her dress there and then, and, locking her stained one in the suit-case, had driven off. She had gone back to the hotel at Brighton, where she was well known, and had timed her arrival to make her story seem true that she had been detained in town overnight and had made an early start in order to avoid the week-end traffic to Brighton. But the situation got on her nerves, and later in the morning she decided to return to town, to try and find out if anything were yet known of the murder. She told her maids that she was obliged to come back on business, and was completely taken by surprise when they gave her Mary's message and showed her the suit-case. A little reflection made her deduce what it contained. She herself had not known how to get rid of her clothing, for a suburban garden gave no chance of burying anything without being noticed, and her house, being eminently modern, was heated by gas and electricity and contained no open fire. She waited until she had planned out details and decided what she would do, and had then broken open Mary's case. She had thought out a plan of action, and really determined there and then that she would go to Inspector Woods with her tale. James Murray had agreed to her plan of action. Possibly he would have been unable to save Mary from Eleanor's fierce hatred even had he wished. In any case, he could only do so by confessing his own guilt and Eleanor's. Actually, an intense determination to live was the chief force actuating him. He clung to the life and to the position which were so dreadfully threatened. He believed Mary must, in the end, denounce him, but he and Eleanor had soon convinced themselves she could prove nothing—it was only her word against James', and, while the evidence could be strengthened against her, the traces of their complicity could be obliterated. The fact that her clothes were bloodstained must tell heavily against her. She had been persuaded to take Helen's jewellery, which, in all probability, could be traced to her if she had followed James' suggestion and tried to sell it. Owing to the fact that James Murray was alone in the house for the week-end, he had plenty of time to remove any signs of his or Eleanor's presence. He wiped the fireside axe to remove finger-prints. He wiped out the basin, which both Mary and he had handled, for the same reason. Some of the stains on the floors of both rooms were made by his and by Eleanor's feet, and showed traces of the shoes they had worn. He had therefore given a great deal of attention to them, and had washed the carpets carefully. The sitting-room, where Eleanor's prints betrayed her presence, he had found difficult to do, as the carpet was a light one, and, in consequence, he had gone over it several times, and had been obliged to give a final wash early on the Monday morning, thus leaving it damp. The rug with Mary's footprints he had deliberately left, salving his conscience by saying that, in all probability, the police would never trace the prints to her, while they would effectively divert suspicion from himself. He had burnt his stained shirt, and had wished to burn his suit. But he soon realized that coat, waistcoat, and trousers would have to be entirely burnt up, and this was not only difficult to achieve but would leave such traces in the ash as might attract the attention of the daily woman. That he dared not risk, nor could he see how to get rid of his boots, which were deeply stained and which must betray him if investigation were made. He dared not try to bury the things in the garden, lest the gardeners should notice, or the police, when the murder should be discovered. In the end neither he nor Eleanor could think of any better plan than to lock both his and Eleanor's things in her strongest suit-case and consign it to her boxroom, where it seemed in the highest degree unlikely any search would be made. The key of Helen's sitting-room he had carried about with him all the fatal week-end, while he was cleaning up the rooms. He had kept it in his pocket on the Monday, and then, realizing the police would search the house, had thought it best to conceal it with his clothes. 'If they're found, we're done for anyway,' he had remarked.

"Then, after the first shock had passed, had come the inevitable realization how much the crime placed these two in each other's power. They were bound together by their guilt, and for both of them everything depended on the ability of the other to avoid arousing suspicion and to stand firm if, by any chance, attention were drawn to them. Successful concealment of guilt in the face of cross-examination is not easy even for one person; where two are involved it becomes immeasurably more difficult. All recorded instances of crimes where two persons have been charged prove this, and it was not long before this man and woman began to realize how much each had to dread from the other. James, in especial, mistrusted Eleanor's self-control, for he knew now how violent and unstable was her disposition. He saw that her nerve was shaken, and he dreaded lest police attention should, by any chance, be directed towards her. He believed that, if forced to give evidence and cross-examined, she would break down. He had no such fears as to his own ability to stand examination. Jack Spens' plea that, as a husband, he could not be made to give evidence against his wife, seemed to show James a way to safety. He knew he had been suspected by the police, and he felt he was the more likely of the two to be accused. He had therefore suggested marriage to Eleanor, who, in her turn, saw the advantages of such a course and who, in her shaken state, could not stand up against Murray's determination. Spurred on by this plan of action, she had adopted the attitude of friendliness which had so pleasantly surprised Glenda and Alan and had been able to arrange conversations with James. Both hoped they had paved the way to marriage without unnecessary comment being aroused.

"They had not reckoned on the persistence of the Inspector's suspicions and uneasiness, which had caused him to remain on the alert.

"That visit from the Registrar made everything fall into place in my brain," said Woods. "I heard from him that Mr. Murray had given notice of a immediate marriage between himself and Miss Spens. It struck me at once, why should Mr. Murray wish to marry at this stage? Miss Glenda was old enough now to be able to take Miss Bailey's place and run 'The Towers' for him. Again, why should Miss Spens think of connecting herself with such an unpleasantly notorious family? She'd money enough; she'd got her brother back; her sister-in-law was safely landed in gaol with a life-sentence. I felt convinced this hasty marriage was the sign of a guilty secret between her and James.

"Moreover, when I looked back, I'd always distrusted the part Miss Spens had played in calling attention to her sister-in-law. When she came to see me, her tale of the suit-case was plausible enough. But I knew as well as she did the motive for her action was hatred of Mrs. Spens. I'd seen she had strong feelings, and of a hostile kind. I felt she'd be a ruthless enemy, and again I saw how that fitted in. Revenge and hatred will make people do things that surprise them in their better moments.

"Then, thinking on these lines, I wondered whether Miss Spens could possibly be the person I'd surmised behind James. She was a friend of the Murrays, knew the house, and might have called there that night. Could I get any other light? I found she'd a car garaged at Highstead, and went straight off myself to have a look at it. I saw at once she had one foreign tyre, fitted on when she'd been abroad in June. I had the track of the car tested, and shown to young Rawlings. When he recognized it for the one he'd seen at 'The Towers' that 8th July, I knew I was right.

"Going on from there, I asked myself, Had Miss Spens taken James' clothes away; were they hidden in her house, and could I hope to find them?

"Of course, when it came to the question of searching her house, I realized what a risk I was taking. I was gambling on my own beliefs.

Actually I did know nothing had been destroyed there, and I had to go by what I knew of Miss Spens. I had always realized she was a woman of great determination and of a high level of intelligence. I put myself in her place. I remembered the saying, 'When a man wants to hide a leaf, he will conceal it in a forest.' If she wanted to hide a fair-sized bundle of stained clothing, she'd naturally put in a box. And where would be the best place for a box? Why, the boxroom, of course. And, therefore, I instructed Riley to search her suit-cases and her boxroom first of all."

"But I still don't know how you dared," objected his uncle. "That marriage might have been perfectly normal, and, if you'd searched that house and found nothing, you'd have been broken. Mr. Murray would have seen to that."

"Well," said Woods. "I think that, after all, one is often guided by the opinion one forms of character. I'd had plenty of opportunity of knowing Mary Spens was a gentle creature; feeling her position most terribly; quite crushed by finding herself in the dock. She didn't make me feel she had the resolution to carry through such a crime, and I became more and more doubtful of her guilt as time went on. Miss Eleanor produced just the opposite effect. I sensed she was hard and determined, and quite capable of planning and ruthlessly carrying out a course she'd set her mind on. When the time came, I had to decide one way or the other. If I kept quiet, that marriage would go through and perhaps with it the last hope of solving the mystery. And that meant Mary Spens would spend the best part of her life as a convict, and you and I both knew what that would mean to a girl like her. Anyway, I had no personal hesitation; I was determined to take the risk. One tiny detail settled the matter for me. I'd made the inquiries myself, most cautiously, and when I went privately to her house I managed to find out from her maids how she'd had out her suit-cases lately and gone through the boxroom, and I thought to myself, 'Those things are there, and she means to take them with her on her honeymoon.' So I risked it, and instructed Riley to go straight in and search directly she and Murray had started for the Registry. He found the case, put with her other luggage in the hall, ripped it up—and not only were Murray's things there, but hers as well—the dress splashed and stained and the sleeves soaked with blood. He rang me up, and, as you know, I was able to arrest them as they arrived at the office. I'd not too much evidence against them, but what I had was conclusive. Then, what James had feared, came about. Eleanor's nerve broke and, as you know, when she gave evidence at the trial, she couldn't keep it up. She couldn't shield James and she couldn't account for her clothes as Mrs. Spens could. In fact, her efforts right to the last to keep the guilt fixed on her sister-in-law led her into hopeless lies. The jury didn't attempt to believe her, and so she and he got their deserts."

There was a brief pause while both men thought of that couple, defiant and untouched by any remorse to the very last.

"And what will happen to Mrs. Spens now?" inquired Uncle James.

"Free pardon," said Woods briefly. "But it'll be a long time before she'll get over what she's been through and suffered. She'll have to do as the Murrays have done—change her name and go abroad. It's been a nasty case altogether."

"Well, I don't know," said Uncle James cheerfully, feeling he had had an enjoyable evening with full information from the fountain-head. "You might say it was an excellent case, for in it you had all the regular motives we're always told to look for in a murder case—only here they're all present, not only one—money—woman—and revenge."

"Look at it like that, if you choose," retorted Woods sarcastically. "To my mind it's been a beastly affair from start to finish."